U

Gate-fold … so marvellou… and buttocks … ung ladies in … ger. Their circumstances were a health hazard. They ran a grave risk of head-colds, caught from the inside up.

'What the –' I spluttered, and then I remembered. Stephen wasn't being self-indulgent: he was relieving Mafeking, bringing the news from Ghent to Aix. Adult magazines for the sex-starved boys in Brisbane . . .

I relinquished my ire and my sick bag and started rummaging through my papers. *Somewhere* I must have that male prostitute's address.

Also by Alida Baxter in *Star*

FLAT ON MY BACK
UP TO MY NECK
DON'T HANG UP SOPHIE – IT'S GOD
TWO'S COMPANY

For children

EMMIE AND THE WITCH'S BUTTON

UPSIDE-DOWN UNDER

Alida Baxter

Illustrated by Bill Tidy

A STAR BOOK
published by
the Paperback Division of
W. H. ALLEN & Co. Ltd

A Star Book
Published in 1979
by the Paperback Division of
W.H. Allen & Co. Ltd
A Howard and Wyndham Company
44 Hill Street, London W1X 8LB

First published in Great Britain by W.H. Allen & Co. Ltd, 1978

Printed in Great Britain by
Richard Clay (The Chaucer Press) Ltd
Bungay, Suffolk

ISBN 352 303565

This book could be dedicated to Robert Sommerhalder, the dear man whose company took me *down* to Australia.

Or to Paul MacNamara, the dear man whose company flew me *around* Australia.

But it is dedicated to Leigh Knights, because *his* company flew me *back*.

Acknowledgements

If it weren't for the following people, this book would never have been written. Now you know who to blame.

Firstly, my Mother. For not having a nervous breakdown.

Next, the Far East Travel Centre. For allowing me to sample their Jet-Ship service, a marvellously enjoyable, comfortable and interesting method of getting from England to Australia. The opportunity to arrive horizontal was one for which I shall ever be grateful.

Then, Trans Australia Airlines. For flying me everywhere within that vast continent on time, with the minimum of fuss, the maximum of courtesy and kindliness, and without once, *ever,* losing my luggage.

Audrey and Alex Faiman of Rical Enterprises, and all their family of distributors in Australia and Ian Crysell of WBD in New Zealand. For looking after me so well and for taking endless time and trouble in order to make me feel welcome and happy and at home, even when I may have been none of those things!

Babette Johnson in Sydney and Barry McFadyen in Melbourne. For helping me enormously, when I most needed it.

The Australian Tourist Commission. For providing me with so much good material.

Stephen Howe. For managing to be always good-humoured, always sensible and always *there* for three whole states, while I stumbled round radio stations putting my foot in everything.

Henry Kitchen. For help, advice, encouragement and rescue-work beyond the call of any publisher's duty. *And* for supplying handkerchiefs and waterproof shoulders.

Mr and Mrs Brian Ludlam, and Mrs Doreen, in Adelaide. For taking in an hysteric, running a convalescent home, and acting as full-time, unpaid secretaries and hand-holders.

Kevin Rasheed and his family, everyone at Wilpena

Pound, and most especially Maureen. For showing me what throughout my trip I always hoped to find – a landscape and a quality of beauty that were totally unique. It would be impossible to do justice to their friendliness or their surroundings, but I have tried.

The Kaiser Stuhl Winery. For enormous hospitality which I remember through a fog of alcohol. And Keith Norton-Smith and his wife and daughters, for making me laugh even when I was sober.

The Singapore Tourist Board, and particularly Madeleine and Simon. For their energy, enthusiasm and wit, and for taking care of me in Singapore, where I spent some of the most unforgettably greedy days of my life.

Singapore Airlines. For flying me all the way home from New Zealand in truly incredible comfort and luxury, and for proving that it is possible to run a Grand Hotel at no matter how many thousand feet.

And, lastly, the gentleman back home in England. For the letters and telephone calls which were a constant source of support, strength and encouragement to me when I felt very English and very unfunny indeed.

To all of these people, my love and gratitude. To some of them, very large kisses. They all shared my life for a time.

After I got back, I read something about the Australian:

'He is proud of England, though very generally angry with England because England will not do exactly what he wants.

'He reconciles this to his mind by telling himself that it is the England of the past of which he is proud, and the England of the present with which he is angry.'

I wish to Hell I'd known. But I'm not up to date with my reading. Anthony Trollope wrote that in 1873.

IN-FLIGHT
SPIRIT LEVELS

CHAPTER ONE

So there I was with four people's cushions, flat on my back in a 747. As yet, unfortunately, it's not the only way to fly. I could hear the gnashing teeth of resentful people all round me, and when I opened one eye at them they were travelling sitting up.

I shut the eye briskly. I can't stand the sight of suffering, and besides the other passengers' stares had been as friendly as castrating knives. They looked like accusing rabbits in some frightful, inhuman experiment, forced to sit up and hear things at a height of thirty thousand feet. Plastic flex tethered them by the ears to the in-flight amusement, and thank God they'd had to pay real money to be tied down. This meant, I hoped, I was safe from attack for the moment. Having paid for plastic food the English will grimly refuse to vomit. Having paid for plastic dialogue they wouldn't unplug their stethoscopes if it meant going down with the 'plane.

I risked a quick glance through my lashes. The rabbits were red-eyed and restive. Before the movie started they were being fed Tijuana Brass. I could hear it without being plugged in, so I presumed the volume was loud. There was a good deal of rustling and shifting, and they didn't look very happy with their intravenous enjoyment. Certainly not as happy as the boys at the back of the 'plane.

The boys at the back of the 'plane were crouched in the aisles with their beer cans, out-swearing each-other and talking to knees on good legs. They'd set up their makeshift encampment unhurriedly, straight after take-off, and if it meant having to stand up they'd never get round to good breasts. They were more comfortable crouching. They were Australians.

Each to his own. I stretched out, callous, ignoring the envious rabbits. Four whole seats to myself! I'd leaned on my back with the steward (using your front counts as tipping) and from time to time he sat by my head and asked me how I was. He'd helped me defend my position, and lying flat to eat my dinner had fortified the stronghold. It had also given me terrible wind — with four seats you get suffering. My pain-killers clattered like castanets in a spin-drier and a rabbit stared at me, hypnotised. I stared back, unaffected. After all (I kicked a child, who'd attempted to sit on my ankle) they ought to be sympathetic; these beasts didn't have my problem. *They* hadn't done something awful bending over to shut a suitcase.

I *had* to lie flat, that's what I'd told the steward, and now here I was, a perfect line (he'd got out a spirit level), flat on my back from my head to my feet.

A woman appeared, cross-faced and accusatory, over my toes. She was trying to find somewhere spare for her small daughter. (Miss Squat 1978. Preparing to be a beautiful stump.) Her daughter might be small, but that didn't mean she wouldn't understand the movie. *She must not be denied that movie* — and the seat with my toes in it had the best view of the screen.

My pain-killers rattled. *That!* Miss Squat on my insteps with her plastic stethoscope!

'Madam,' I said unevenly (it's hard to speak evenly when you're lying down). 'I can't move my feet because I'll have an awful pain. And your daughter will have a worse pain if she tries to take that seat!'

Perhaps I could have been nicer. But then, if I'd been nicer, I wouldn't have kept four whole seats.

I closed my eyes firmly on Stump and her mother and the blurred titles — all I wanted now was to be allowed to sleep. The mere opening moments of the movie made me drowsy; if only I had this at home I'd never need Tranxene. 'Won Ton Ton – The Dog Who Saved Hollywood'. And there were people who were paying to sit up all night and watch it. What in God's name was I travelling with? It was lonely, being sane.

I twitched sleepily, and snivelled, and pummelled a couple of pillows into the shape of a much-missed back. The disembodied pilot told me what the local time was, and I wondered blearily where the local was where all the time went on.

And what the Hell I was doing, going down under anyway.

CHAPTER TWO

It was to do with books and money. Everything in my life is to do with books and money. If it isn't to do with men. Even the men in my life are to do with books and money. I sit around talking about money and they sit around talking about books.

The talking about books this time had got round to my next one, and the fact that I should go on writing down the things that happened to me.

Now usually I'm pretty light-hearted about the next one, because I don't need to worry – I'll be dead before it starts. Gangrene set in while I was working on the last one, my healthy flush is due to alcoholism and consumption, and the reason I'm eating for two is I have this little growth. But even I flinched back and almost cracked my brandy glass.

Write what happened to me? *Now?* After the divorce action? When every time I shook an old coat, out fell someone's husband?

Every man I knew was gay, or someone else's husband.

And some of them were both.

Even my ex-husband was someone else's husband.

The table rocked and my knees knocked. Somewhere near at hand I heard the thud of falling writs.

'I think –' I said blindly (my contact lenses weren't coping – it was the sweat of fear running in my eyes) 'I'd better go away, you know. Somewhere rather *far* away,' (beyond extradition for libel) 'and do a sort of *travel* book.'

'Where were you thinking of going?'

'Where they won't buy the translation. Ireland. America.'

It was going to be Bangkok – but then they had a crisis. And I didn't fancy the title – my Mother goes through enough.

By a process of elimination (no snow-shoes and drinkable water) it became the Antipodes.

'Thank God!' I told a friend. 'I'll be able to say what I like now. They drink beer and do things to sheep there – everyone knows they can't *read.*'

'Are you sure?'

I frowned at the receiver. 'If they saw a book they'd just shear off the jacket!'

'Well, if you're sure . . .'

The publishers said that they were hoping to sell my books there. I rang back my friend and he said that proved I must be right. And then I met an Australian at a party, and he liked my books because they had pictures in. I found all of this extremely reassuring. Like my publishers.

'When you get down there we'll arrange some promotion, and you can meet the local people – marvellous crowd.'

Marvellous – who needs it?

For free food, drink and accommodation, I'd have met the Transylvanians at Castle Dracula. I was so broke I'd have to pay for the trip with blood.

I took my veins along to a vast Australian airline.

'Yes,' said a tall, lean, urbane man. 'Sounds just the sort of project we should be interested in. Put the proposal in writing, some publisher's authentication, I'll post it all down to Sydney – you leave the whole thing to me.'

'You mean you might help me?' I was grovelling with my legs crossed, so desperately anxious to please that I'd unbuttoned my blouse to the thigh.

'Can't promise anything, it'll be up to Head Office. But

the book's to be about Australia . . .' He stared at the window, adjusted his socks, studiously avoided my cleavage. Ended weakly: 'I don't see why not.'

My heart pounding visibly with gratitude and frostbite, I bowed my way out backwards to put it to him in writing. He'd given me great lists – the names and numbers of useful people. And the publisher's had told me that if I didn't leave till May, someone of theirs would be with me, on a coincidental sales tour. Suddenly, in wet and wintry London, the research for this book seemed a good idea.

Not so much good, of course, as essential. 'What the Hell am I going to write?' I asked the receiver. 'What the Hell am I going to say about a desert?'

'They drink beer and do things to sheep and they're illiterate. You told me that yourself.' said my long-suffering friend.

'That's not the country, Martin, that's the Australians! I've seen them – I've been on the Tube going through Earls Court. But how can I –'

'Well, I don't know why you're worried.'

'Oh, don't you! Try being funny about a desert. That's all they've got out there, and sheep, and billabongs!'

'*You* should worry!' Martin was getting huffy. 'I've been asked for a comedy script by the BBC.'

'But that's marvellous –'

'No, it isn't. A working-class comedy! How can I write that? I don't even know what time they eat!'

I consulted the list I'd been given by the man at the airline. Where could I go for some free good advice?

I took my veins along to the Australian Tourist Commission.

'Oh-hoh!' said a bucolic, jolly, large man. 'Get you in a mining camp – how long are you staying?'

'At least four weeks.' I flourished my neckline proudly. Nothing superficial about me. *Or* my researches. No, nothing cursory. If a job was worth doing . . . He must be quite impressed, not having to deal with a fly-by-night.

He was tugging at an earlobe, as though he hadn't heard me. He sorted through his brochures, selected one, cracked its spine. Then he chuckled. 'Funny! I thought you said – *how* long?'

'Four weeks?'

'Four *weeks*?' He sagged, flabbergasted, over his guidebook. 'What d'you expect to see in that time? Haven't you got *any* idea how big the country is?'

Unable to answer, I glanced guiltily at the huge wall-map of his homeland. It did look big. God, it looked big. I gulped, and straightened my shoulders. Perhaps it wasn't *that* big. Perhaps the map was large scale. Over in one corner was a comparison map of Great Britain. It looked like one of those little fish that live off the fleas on a whale.

I tried one of my most winning smiles. The winning smile bounced right off him and fell down and died in a heap.

'You see, I don't know quite how long I'll take to get out there. My publishers want me to make a stop in New Zealand, either on the way out or on the way back. Then, when I arrive, there'll be at least two weeks' promotion . . . As it is, the trip's going to take me about two months. All I can really spare is four weeks in the middle. I just don't see how I can stay away any longer – the book's got to be written and I won't start it till I'm home.'

There was a silence on his part, except for rustling. He was wringing brochures from the dregs of his jollity.

I ventured: 'I'm afraid I don't know very much about Australia –' and was stricken by a shaft from an agonised red eyeball. I swallowed my saliva to build up my strength, and then blundered on again: 'That's why I thought it best to come to you! You can tell me where to go.'

The large Australian controlled himself.

'You know the places to go – the places to see. The whole country can't be desert. It isn't, is it? Australia must have *some* parts of interest?'

His hands tightened convulsively on his brochures; he'd been having a lovely day till I walked in.

'I mean . . .' I floundered. 'Where I can talk to people. Sheep-shearing stations?' His eyeballs paled. 'Billabongs? Bondi Beach?' He uttered a cry.

'No! Concentrate on one state, that's all you'll have time for.' He thrust across the tattered, wasp-waisted brochures. 'South Australia's beautiful — fruit growing area. And the grapes — thank God, the grapes. You can see the wineries!' He mopped his brow with a map. 'You'll see, they'll look after you. They're going to have to. My God, the Barossa Valley — they'll pour you out of there. Leave it to me and I'll draw up a suggested itinerary. Come back in a few weeks, when I've heard from Sydney.'

He ushered me out, the latch clicked and I heard him collapse against the door.

CHAPTER THREE

The aeroplane sat on the tarmac like a man with his arms in plaster, and I dozed and protected myself through the bustle of dawn at Bahrain.

People cleaned around me, agitated in turbans, pouncing on crumpled seat-backs and paper handkerchiefs. They clamoured at one another, vociferous and resentful, unable to gouge out four ashtrays for the sprawl of my arms, knees and feet. Why was I there at all? Why hadn't I roused with the rest of the British? There was a reupholstering of seats — the ones so helpfully vacated while their occupants went for a stroll. Cushions were ransacked for dirt, aerosols dealt with the fumigation, someone tore down a lavatory within inches of my ears. I covered my nose with a scarf and rammed my earplugs in farther, till they remoulded sideways and blocked off my sinuses. This airport didn't attract me: a pink-lit dusty depot with bunches of flaccid palm trees. Staffed by stay-at-home Arabs: the ones who weren't pouring oil on the pound or building sand banks in Park Lane.

It was unclubbable, being lethargic. The main, energetic contingent had trooped out into the morning — though not to look at the landscape or the after-birth of the sunrise. They had found a handy Mecca at the Duty-Free Shop in Bahrain. A reciprocal trade agreement (with the wool counters at Marks & Spencer's?) had made it almost viable as a last resting place for sterling. The Shop personnel restrained themselves and didn't laugh at fivers — presumably they'd come in handy for odd bus-fares in the West End.

Blue turbans bobbed and waggled when I crooked one knee up. An Arab rummaged for a genie in a plastic bag.

Groggy with pain-killers, Marzine and packing, I tucked pillows in my pregnable areas and fell fast asleep.

It must have been a phase when God used his binoculars. Very far-sighted of Him, to have my trip postponed. A bit of Almighty vision — it certainly wasn't me. I'm so near-sighted I can't see to take the milk in. Even if I can find the bottles, I can never find the fridge. And putting off the project was a stroke of Fate with a silver lining. It not only turned out to be vital; it had very fulfilling effects.

Originally I'd planned to travel early in the New Year, but that was before I got cold feet about Bangkok. So of course it was before Australia won the election, *and* before my publishers began having bright ideas.

It was also before the Autumn, when I heard I'd got a flat. From September to January, I'd had the Blitz, the National Debt and the Russian Revolution. BIG THINGS were happening. If I'd gone anywhere in the New Year, it would have been by hearse.

There had been chilly months of sandpapering the builder, blowing up at the Gas Board, having deliveries of kittens and throwing myself, grovelling, on the mercy of the bank. (They knew me very well in there — that's where I went to make phone calls.)

From the trouble it entailed, you'd have thought it was a mansion. What I'd actually got was a flat so small I called it the Wendy House.

'You can't live here!' said a friend of mine, showing me his tape-measure. 'Not possibly, Alida. There's no room for a double bed!' It was true. In fact there was hardly room for a single. Wherever I stood I could touch the walls. *With my elbows bent.*

'Don't worry, what's the difference? It'll be just like

when I was married. There's no law that says because I'm divorced I can't go on sleeping alone!'

He tripped in mid-step, he stopped pacing out: 'Who's worried about the sleeping? Two foot eleven . . . Oh, my God. What about the moving around?'

My friends are exceptionally thoughtful. They always think a lot of my love-life. This one (an overburdened confidant) was geriatric well before his time.

'Alida, be reasonable! A three-foot single? What d'you suppose you're going to do in that? You know you run a mile from the missionary position! How far d'you think you'll be able to run in here?' He gestured and hurt his right hand on the window. His left hand had collided fiercely with the door. 'And where the Hell are you going to put the mirrors? This place is so old they'd pull the plaster down!'

'All I ever said was I *like* mirrors. I didn't tell you they were *imperative.*'

About mirrors, I was prepared to listen to reason. Ever since a girl I knew with an old flat had fixed a mirrored ceiling over her bed. As she said herself, the tragedy could have been avoided if she was the type who lies back and grits her teeth. Instead she makes a noise like an urgent siren and she makes it such a lot that she scares her cat.

The night the blokes upstairs gave their little party, she was hitting Top C and missed the first splintering. Knowing her, she probably missed the second splintering and the rumbling, because the lot fell down on her and her married lover, and it gave them the biggest bang they'd ever had.

I'd still love to have heard the explanation that man gave for some of those cuts when he got home.

'Mirrors,' I repeated, 'are not imperative! To Hell with the plaster, to Hell with the size — what I need is a home!'

And, in order to get a home, I also needed people. Very special people.

People who need people, when the people they need

LONDON CONTRACEPTIVE GLASS Co. LTD.

are plumbers, are not and never feel like the luckiest people in the world.

From September to January I needed plumbers and carpet-layers, gas men and decorators, furniture, fixtures and fittings and a hot line to the GPO.

I wanted so much so soon it was domestic nymphomania. Promiscuity on that scale had predictable results: when I waited for them they didn't arrive but when I wasn't there, they came.

Men tramped through my Wendy House with copper pipe and U-bends, only showing me estimates so they could give me the kiss of life.

Amateurs appeared, all smiles, with zeal and Black and Deckers, hung up things at angles, struck cement and broke their bits.

Professionals peered in and probed, with gloom and awful warnings, and used my flat for interviews (*and* my phone, once it was in).

Fitters came before gas stoves and layers came before carpets, and bills and accounts and invoices came before anything. After omnipresent hysterics I got the impedimenta, and then, like heartburn, I got the fitters and layers back again. They grew to know one another, they had sympathetic discussions, and if I wasn't there to do it, they made each other restorative tea.

Four long frightful months before I saw the last of them, propped the 'Welcome' and the 'Good Luck' cards in a line along the mantelpiece, put some flowers in water and the latch down on the door. January, and I'd finally taken over the Wendy House. It was the last time I took over anything; from that moment onwards, everything overtook me.

CHAPTER FOUR

First, not a thing but a person. And the take-over was conducted with a velvet glove over *force majeure*. There was a bid, a seizure of assets and seismographs everywhere recorded the merger.

I'd been in the flat precisely six days and God knows how I'd lasted that long. Whatever the decorators had hung on my walls, it was impregnated with musk. Men called in shifts, and then they never shifted. For the first time in seven years I had that special something — availability.

No husband on his way home, no mother in the kitchen, no room to run far and no — well, not much will power.

And I'd broken up with my last bloke the day before I moved in. No strings attached, except to my Copper Seven.

I had a heady time being courted by various Chairmen of the Board.

Even so, amazingly, the real take-over took six days. I didn't want to be accused of seeming precipitate.

Because my body always cracks down on a little enjoyment, the next thing to take me over was my throat, which was feeling choked. Five courses of ampicillin later, my tonsils were in a fair way to move in on my brain. My glands were enlarged to the point of being vulgar and I was feeling as fed up as my throat.

'Right!' said my doctor. 'I've had enough of this and by the look of it, so have your tonsils.'

The hospital took me over: some brave man would go in there and get my tonsils out.

More to the point, he'd get them out before I went to Australia. It was that or the flying doctor doing a rush job somewhere in the bush.

I trotted home with a swollen head and a Linda Lovelace complex: my throat was so interesting it was a National Health emergency.

And it wasn't the only panic on my enlarged horizon. The vast Australian airline had dithered and dropped me flat. Perhaps they had someone in Sydney (it was, after all, their Head Office) who could decipher letters — who could, to be blunt, *read.* And, one afternoon, roused from his sleep by low-flying pollution, he had actually picked up, flicked through and *read* my books.

Possibly, after instant can-to-mouth resuscitation, he'd managed to gibber questions: if I wrote like that about a husband, what would I do to a Corporation? What would I do to the innocent Australian, going about his business at his happy average slouch?

How could they, in all conscience, let me loose down in Australia — an inoffensive country that did the world no harm. It just lay there, making butter. Letting sheep run over it. Giving people a suntan and irrigating itself with beer.

They had enough trouble already, with their exported image. What did they have representing them in the Northern Hemisphere? Edna Everidge, who appeared on the stage and television, acting as though Melbourne ladies discussed their husbands' colostomies. A man who dressed as a woman and waved at people with Gladioli! No, they'd be crazy to give me a lift, they already had trouble enough.

Alternatively, of course, it could have been that the airline had run out of contra deals.

When I'd stopped screaming and taking aspirin I looked through my wardrobe and took off my bra. I had to get to Australia and I didn't have any money — that had been spent on the flat. Women in my situation need a generous benefactor. My benefactor was generous but he wasn't a nationalised airline, and he didn't want me to go anyway.

I put on my pneumonia neckline and the stockings that stayed up by themselves.

I also put in my handbag the publisher's letters and other credentials — and I got taken over again.

There were people who proved willing to help me get down to Australia! None of them, intriguingly, were Australian nationals. I'd be flown to Singapore; I'd be put on a ship to Fremantle; I'd be flown around Australia; I'd be flown back via Singapore.

The companies smiled parentally and patted handy parts of me. They were only too happy to help with the book, they were looking forward to it, was there anything else they could do?

I was looking forward to it. I was looking forward to any book that wasn't the one I was working on. There'd been yet another take-over, and there wasn't that much of me left. This time it was the characters, which was hard luck on my neighbours: the leading lady was an American and she shouted and tap-danced a lot.

I smiled ingenuously at the kind companies and patted their wallets of tickets. Anything they could do for me? Perhaps they could write me a book.

Quite extraordinary: I had no offers to take over that.

CHAPTER FIVE

We were lifted away from our stomachs and served them up with our breakfast.

Passengers, twelve hours weaker now, tore ineptly at limpet tinfoil. I wasn't any weaker, but I was still horizontal, and it took me from Bahrain to Dubai to grapple the wraps off the food. The struggle was hardly worth it: I ate half of a crusty roll before realising it was a lid.

People roused and shifted, jet-lagged at last and sluggish, queueing at the lavatories and then settling down again.

I lifted my head cautiously and took a look around me. I wanted to go and clean my teeth (to judge by the smells, a unique manoeuvre) but I had to do that and get back again before someone pinched all my seats. Bodies lolled like broken dolls. The rear throbbed with snores and Australian slobbers. The cabin was a castle of sleeping uglies — I might even have time for a wash!

I wrapped up soap and a flannel, toothpaste, toothbrush, a change of underwear . . . And I could stand up without wincing! The hours spent flat on my back had done wonders for my problem.

Sneaking along the aisles, I tripped over the pursed lips of a shrewd-eyed, wide-awake lady. She narrowed at what I had in my hands and I looked everywhere but at her hair, which was shiny, grey-yellow nylon.

'Boring, isn't it?' Nervous, slightly desperate; the lavatories were all engaged and I sat on the arm of an ugly. He broke wind plaintively. 'I'll be glad to get off the 'plane.'

Her eyes moved: not slits, little pebbles.

'Usually I love flying, but my back went just before the taxi came. I suppose it was bending over, stuffing in that hairbrush.'

Her eyes moved: not little pebbles, rocks.

Still no vacancies. I played aimlessly with my flannel. After Singapore, we'd probably never meet again. I forced myself not to stare at the hypnotic nylon. Why explain to Rock Eyes about taking the suitcase down off the fridge? I'd had to keep one there – there'd been nowhere else in the Wendy House for it – and I'd climbed up with necessities, and a kitchen stool, to pack. Never a moment's trouble, whether I was in high heels or bedroom slippers or bare footed. But then I'd taken the case down. And found a hairbrush, at the very last minute. And stooped to stow it – and finally gone too far. Something in my back had snapped.

'Thank goodness I'm going on by ship, from Singapore to Fremantle.'

Her eyes moved: not rocks now, small boulders.

'It'll be nice, just to be able to stretch my legs.'

She laughed nasally. I might have mentioned a public hanging. 'Stretch your legs where? Going from your bunk to the tut?'

'Er – ah –'

'Five days and all I'll want's a bunk. Would you believe that I looked good when I left Wollongong?'

'Well, you don't look –'

'If my family knew! I'm not telling anybody.' The boulders had grown, she was obviously telling me. 'And I'd been looking forward to seeing round London. I'd been going to stay for the Jubilee. How could you leave England for the Jubilee? I didn't have my strength left. They beat me away from the dining room with their sticks!'

'My God!' Understandably, the ugly whose arm I was

sitting on flinched.

'I went over on the *Can-berra!* You know the *Canberra?*'

'Not intimately.'

'I was ready to throw myself off the ship!'

'But I thought the *Canberra* —'

'There's nothing wrong with the *Can-berra!*' An adenoidal trill. 'It wasn't the ship, it was the people they had on board!'

'Yes, I am a bit worried,' I ventured. 'About this business of sharing —'

'I shared a cabin with a sick woman and I nearly died! If my family knew — they came up the gangplank on crutches!'

'Your family?'

'No, those people on the *Can-berra!* They were taking some kind of sea-trip for their health!' The boulders receded slightly. 'Thank God I'll soon be home.'

'Yes.' I didn't know what to say. I was just starting out on my own journey. Homesick already, I struggled for optimism. 'But whatever this ship's like, we'll only be on it for five days.'

The boulders smouldered. 'Five days can be Hell.'

But surely not on *that* boat. It glistened white in the Singapore sunshine, it fluttered with little, bright-coloured scraps like the bottom halves of bikinis. It seethed with scurrying porters and was reassuringly *small.*

'My goodness. Good Heavens,' said Hester. 'And I thought we'd go out on a lighter. You can stop worrying, Alida. We won't lose each other on that.'

I clutched at her cape-hem and nodded. At the airport we'd blundered together and joined like Rugby goal-posts. Both very tall and short-sighted, we could help one another find pavements, and had spent the previous evening hopping across Monsoon drains. My senior, Hester was more cautious, and more sceptical of male strollers. 'Never look round!' she'd said grimly. For me, an impossible assignment: when I'm thin I still never look flat.

We had watched the dry-storm lightning, and peered through fences at crumbling Maugham mansions, and listened to tooting car-horns and industrious cicadas. Singapore was Kew Gardens, after the stars come out.

Alone later, in my vast silky hotel suite, I gazed dreamily over the sky-line. Just the night for my package from home. I would play the fond words recorded by my kind-hearted left-behind lover. He'd taken it very well, really. He hadn't *really* been grumpy. His last, parting gift was a tape. Something to warm me and cheer me. Full of trust, I switched on the machine.

Four months by then that I'd known him. Four months, and he'd concealed his sadistic tendencies. The most comforting thing he'd recorded was a poem with only six deaths. As light relief, him reading *'If I should die, think only this of me . . .'* Five minutes of heart-break, and my cassette was awash.

I turned off the rusting player and swiftly switched on the TV. Singapore had all-night undubbed *Star-Trek!* I swallowed pain-killers and hot milk and drooled at a young Richard Johnson. Either it was a very old episode or Customs had de-bagged his eyes.

Hester was watching the luggage and hoping we'd share a cabin. I'd given up hoping, and prayed. The motley assortment of travellers humping their traps up the gangplank were hardier, and noisier, and a Hell of a lot fitter than me. They hadn't gone bright pink, like I had. Their hair hadn't sat down, like mine had. They'd never be sea-sick, like I would (but I can get sea-sick in baths). Hester was protective and I prayed she'd share my cabin. She'd look after me and protect me from the water and lavatory seats. She was a grandmother who commuted all the way from the Northern Hemisphere, and her idea of an outing was a short stop off in Tibet. She was also in love with somebody, which gave us much Kleenex in common, and was full of handy hints on how to deal with Aussies.

'Never criticise *anything,* they're so defensively touchy, and don't be surprised at how new it all is. They haven't had time to get old.'

This did not seem to be true of the women, most of whom had faces like the San Andreas Fault. Now that I'd seen some of them, I was swelling with sympathy for the poor Australian men.

A group of these bedevilled, defenceless specimens (only seven feet tall — surely rickets in childhood) had directed me to Change Alley when I wanted to buy a camera. They were immensely polite and helpful. They'd have *taken* me to Change Alley, if they'd been able to stand up.

'Ah, yes,' sighed Hester. 'Winsome people, the Australians. Quite fascinating . . . Just look at that one, there.'

That one there was Rock Eyes, who'd gone auburn without her wig. She was cracking her tongue at porters and searching them for her luggage. Since the luggage was being swung in great hair-nets from the quay-side, her ransacking and remonstrances were doing not the slightest bit of good.

I made her known to Hester, and destinations were exchanged. 'I can't recall exactly —' Hester dabbed her forehead vaguely. 'the name of the village where my daughter lives . . .'

'Village? Village!' Rock Eyes hissed. She regrouped her crevasses and then put out a laugh. Hester stood her bit of deck but I had cowered back. 'We don't have villages. Hah-hah!' (The laughing hangman.) 'You've got villages in England. In Australia we've got towns.'

'It's a question of semantics.' Slender English fingers adjusted a coil of silver hair. 'Words, you know. Language. Of course I shouldn't have said a village. Your towns are what we call hamlets.'

The ladies smiled divinely. I was watching glaciers

move. The crunch was interrupted by the arrival of a full hair-net, and Rock Eyes returned to her haranguing of the porters. I went back to praying for someone nice to cabin with. Hester, it transpired, had been consigned to the bowels – 'Isn't it awful, m'dear, but I shouldn't have hoped, I'm doing this trip on the cheap' – whilst my gift tokens had projected me to the spacious purlieus of A Deck.

A tiny, scrawny porter fished my cases from the hair-net and I scrambled after him anxiously, into the snakes and ladders ship. Up and over the steps of doorways, past coffee bars and ping-pong tables, the sweep of a curving stairway, a dimly-lit varnished lounge . . .

He plonked my cases in a cabin, grinned at me and vanished. There was a cardigan lying on one bunk (the *best* bunk) already, and I advanced upon it, staring. I was mesmerised. When last seen, this hypnotic garment had been draped around Rock Eyes' shoulders. Out in the harbour the sea was calm; inside the cabin I fought waves of mounting hysteria.

'Well!' barked a voice behind me. 'Not bad for space, is it? We've got enough room to fight.'

I closed my eyes and reopened them, but they were still there – the cabin and cardy. And Rock Eyes, manhandling her luggage. She looked as though she could have moored a liner with one hand.

I had to converse, and try to stop gulping: 'I do hope they don't let down that other bunk.' At my eye-level, along the wall, ran a huge slab of polished wood. 'It's right above where you've left me – where I'll be sleeping. There's only six inches' clearance . . . What on earth'll happen if they have to let that down?'

'Easy,' she said cheerfully. 'Whenever you move you'll hit your head.' She was bouncing experimentally on her bunk beneath the porthole, with its misty, dusky, enchanting view of Singapore. 'Well, it seems to be holding. Wonder if they've changed the sheets.'

'Oh, good God!' I gabbled. 'Surely!' I was kneeling to

stow my luggage beneath my bunk and carry on praying. As I reached into darkness I noticed something: dangling from the mattress was an extremely antique sock.

Wordlessly, I rose and peeled back the bedding and blankets. The sheets and pillows were spotlessly clean.

Reassured, I knelt again. Perhaps down here God would hear me better. Perhaps it would turn out that after all there'd been some nice mistake. Rock Eyes had another cabin – preferably one on shore. I moved my hold-all and a cockroach ran out of it. I followed suit and ran out of my mind.

My cabin-mate sat motionless, like Cleopatra, on her bunk. 'Well,' she said disinterestedly, 'I'm glad it's your bags they're in and not mine.'

'*They?*' I screamed, rattled. I'd recklessly taken a shoe off and was attempting to kill the monster. 'Do you mean there's more than one?'

'Sure to be. Just you keep your bags away from mine, that's all.'

Of course I could have gone for her with the shoe, but I'd only have broken the heel. Instead my spleen had to be vented by alternately banging about under the bunk and leaping hysterically back.

This cabaret was interrupted by a knock at the door which preceded a body. The body was loosely connected to our cabin steward's head. His face was that of a five-year-old who slept well and had come into money. He introduced himself and I, rather nervously, introduced him to the sock.

'Las pass'ges,' he explained. 'Cheerdlun!' The sock was whisked away.

'There is also,' I husked, 'a cockroach.'

'Hwa?'

I made wriggling movements with my fingers, around my bags and along my bunk.

'Hah! I cum an' splay.' He disappeared, brisk and cheery. He was obviously perfectly competent to strangle cockroaches in his cot.

CABIN
COCK LOACH SPLAY
OLD SOCK SPLAY

Rock Eyes had been torpid, thinking. She suddenly said 'I'll be over-run! They get in your bags, they get in your house and you're over-run. I'll have to unpack on the lawn, shake it all out over tissue paper.' This partial solution restored her stoic humour. She said 'Well, if that's where they're nesting I'm glad I haven't got your bunk.'

I glowered at her, murderously, but she'd turned to look through the porthole. If there hadn't been a porthole, one look of hers would have made the hole.

'I'm going up on deck,' she announced. 'Seems as though we're sailing. And we might as well move while we can.'

My cockroach-ridden bunk supported my thighs, which were quivering. My cracking voice asked, 'What do you mean?'

'We're heading for open ocean – and wait till we get near Fremantle! One thing I'll say for Fremantle, they know how to hand out the gales.'

With which bright intelligence, she left me to have my collapse.

Dusk was seeping sootily across the floor of the cabin. Outside the lights of the harbour glistened and slid in a mist. It was a moment that required tortured chords in the background, and what was tonight's orchestration? Cockroaches wearing high-heels!

I sat gingerly on my bunk and listened to their clatter, and the pulsating throb of the engines and the air-conditioning. As usual tears flowed down my face very easily. Slipping away from Singapore in the sultry early evening – why didn't it look like this when you saw it at the Empire?

Sodden and masochistic, I played my cassette in a drizzle and had a therapeutic howl.

Stuck in this cabin with Rock Eyes and at least one of the Plagues of Egypt – she'd been right on the aeroplane, you could see Hell in a week.

CHAPTER SIX

It was around about three in the morning that I finally and fully realised I couldn't bear it any more. I am a *cinq-a-sept* person and back home in my bedroom in London it was nearing zero hour.

Adding weight to my bio-rhythms was a natural requirement, and the fact that I was lying on a hot, vibrating bed. In the midst of that tropic night and drowning in perspiration, I made the grim discovery that a ship's screws are no joke.

No wonder women on liners are said to go potty East of Suez. I couldn't have told you if I was East of Barcelona, but the heat and the vibration and the starry sky through the porthole and the lack of immediate attention were driving me out of my mind.

I held my breath and listened for the wheeze of Rock Eyes' snoring. She didn't snore, she lay there, being Australian and genteel. Was she awake, was she asleep, would she notice, would it matter – with one eye on her solid form, I hazarded an attempt.

Now it has long been a complaint of those nearest and dearest to me that I'm some kind of paraplegic because I can't or won't DIY. During marital separations and marital devastations and post-marital lack of men, I writhed with frustration. It felt like being crawled on by heavy, arthritic ants. I ached from my toes to my pelvis, but *still* I couldn't do it – I had a mental bung. And the problem wasn't just mental: with fingernails the length I wear them, there was the risk of laceration. I suppose I could have cut my nails, but they keep on growing, and before I could get my scissors out something usually turned up.

On the pulsating bunk, with a Hoagie Carmichael night outside the porthole, and at what my body told me was my favourite time of day, nothing was going to turn up but my toes if I didn't hurry. And my nails had got broken packing. I took a grip on myself.

Oh, God, I thought (some time later) men must be bloody clever. When you come to think that they do this instinctively . . . To watch them, you'd think it was easy. With me it was proving as easy as playing the clarinet.

Perhaps I should sleep, and give up.

My bunk went on vibrating, the bright stars went on shining, the sweat collected in tributaries and rills and reservoired in my navel.

Softly, very softly, I beat my head on the wall.

Be calm, I tried to tell myself, lie back and go over your lumps. Relax – wring out your nightie. Close your eyes and think of England.

It was thinking of England that did it. Some extremely revealing minutes passed, and I made a discovery. That involuntary cry you make – it is involuntary. It's unstoppable, it's inexorable and you cannot shut it up.

Hitherto, being much occupied at the moment in question, I had never particularly noticed the amount of noise I make. At three o'clock in the morning, in a shared ship's cabin, with Rock Eyes' state a question and her bunk three feet away, it came upon me with a start that I sounded like Rita Hunter deprived of a cream bun.

But you can't change your mind half-way down a helter-skelter. At no little personal cost, I put my hand firmly over my mouth – and got a bitten thumb.

Was a thumb going to stand between me and my personal Everest? With paranoid precision, I stuffed the sheet between my teeth. Moments later my lips parted, my teeth parted, out fell the sheet and out came the cry. Rita was on form tonight, cream buns and the Valkyrie.

There was a sleepy mutter from Rock Eyes, an upheaval in her bunk — and I lay in my bunk, still gently quivering, and feeling descending upon me a great and dream-bringing peace.

'Funny noise —' (I forced it out.) 'Isn't it, the air-conditioning?' My voice sounded funny to me.

Melodic chimes announced meal-times and each new day brought a new news-sheet. I roused blearily on the first morning to find Rock Eyes with her face on and the sunlight shining blindingly off the water and her false teeth. She had opted for the first sitting, which meant that for an hour at least I had the cabin to myself. Little did I know how I'd come to value this arrangement, bolting down from the deck or the lounge when I heard the first-sitting bell. Rock Eyes and I would pass one another, she going out and I coming in. For an hour I could play with talcum or gargle unobserved. At all other times I had no privacy.

Rock Eyes found my body and all I did to it fascinating, and when I strip-washed or exercised or craned in the mirror to put on mascara she sat watching and making suggestions, apparently riveted to her bunk.

She also demanded comments, especially when dressing for dinner, but her demands were of the dumb-striking kind, like 'Does my wig look real?' Being totally unable to be as frank as she was, I found myself continually and monumentally nonplussed. Nor was I tempted to make any minute or close-up inspections; I didn't find her anatomy as arresting as she found mine.

It wasn't so bad in the beginning, when I was still using the shower, but as the voyage screwed on its way the shower became hazardous. For some unfathomable reason, the hot water gushed hotter and hotter; I wasn't careful when I washed my hair, and I scalded off half my scalp. That evening the Captain confided that he'd been as startled as I was. *He'd* turned on his shower and left it to warm up. Billowing clouds of steam had attracted his

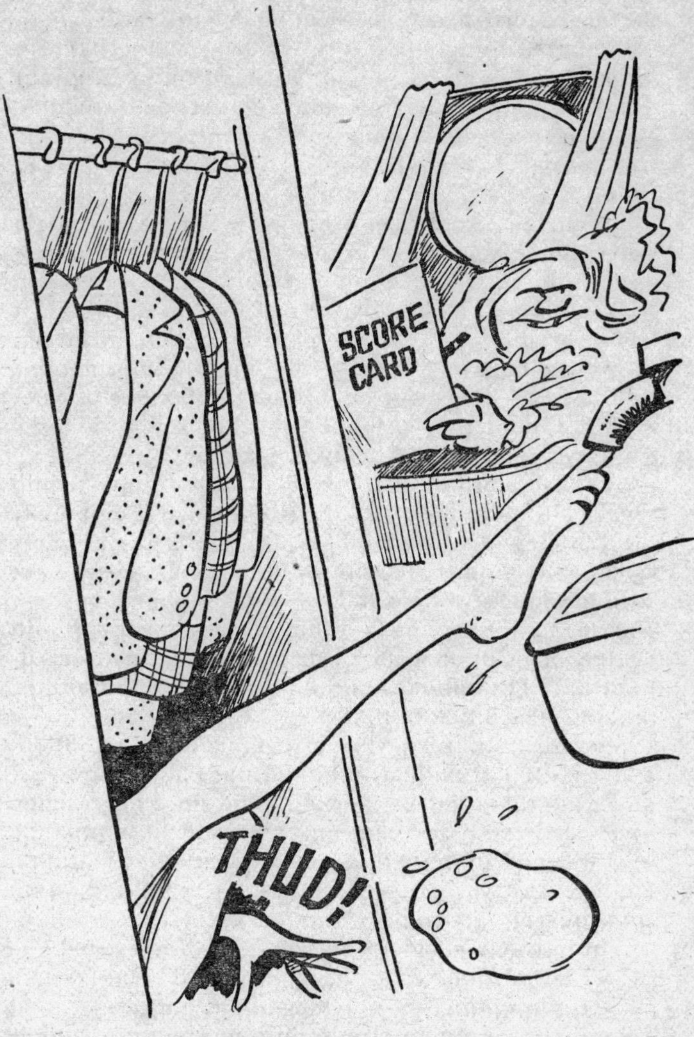
SCORE CARD
THUD!

boggling steward, and the pair of them had spent an hour skidding about on the tiling, trying to get near enough to the taps to turn them off without boiling to death.

I resorted to acrobatic strip-washing at the basin, a move requiring agility in mid-Ocean when washing your feet. The ship would roll and I'd describe a sudden, alarming parabola, cannoning into the door and then ricocheting into a wardrobe with one foot trapped under a tap.

Throughout these performances, Rock Eyes would watch unblinkingly and critical, and since her narrow stare was less than complimentary, I became self-conscious about nudity for the first time in my life. If it hadn't been for the Heaven-sent disparity in our sittings there would have formed about me an impenetrable cloud of BO. Given the opportunity, I became a secret washer. Considering what else I did, I reckon it was lucky Rock Eyes spent most of her nights asleep.

The days formed a fattening pattern, marked into time-spans by chimes. I ate hugely, regularly, unusually silent at meal-times, straining to hear the Captain, whose voice was very quiet. The others gave up completely; *I* got swollen veins listening, and I was at his left hand.

Avoiding the communal cabin, I'd lie sunbathing with Hester, or read, or write, or drink tea in a tiny, tucked-away bar. The imbibing of tea by the gallon had formed part of sealed orders from home.

My throat was still healing after the tonsils' excavation, and I was continually dry. Liquid was poured down my gullet at every available moment, and since my reaction to alcohol is to find someone nice and lie down, the instructions had been firm and explicit: '*Don't* drink a lot, I've seen you after two glasses of wine, and watch those buggers on that boat!'

The instruction had not been entirely disinterested.

So I sat inhaling tea as though it were oil and I were a tanker, surreptitiously watching those buggers on that boat. They were a motley lot of buggers, and I simply couldn't understand what my bloke had been raving about. As far as I could see, they spent their blameless lives lying quietly in the bar. They never appeared at breakfast, but a gentleman from Tasmania told me over my tea-cup that that was because they only woke up when the crew started hosing the deck. Apart from drinking steadily and sleeping where they'd fallen, they seemed to be doing no harm. It did strike me as rather odd that they were in much better shape than the girls.

The girls who had started out on the trip dimpling and sun-kissed and nubile, grew greyer and more vengeful and more exhausted as each day wore on. They shrieked a lot in the small hours and I met them in the ship's shop, buying aspirin. They developed strange rashes of bruises and began to lose track of their clothes. They went for evening strolls round the deck and took two nights to find their way back.

The girls' jumpy behaviour and increasingly haggard appearance seemed to be quite independent, and nothing to do with the boys. The boys, when I stepped over them, appeared to be frighteningly fit. And polite, though drowsy. It took me almost the whole voyage to discover that a gallant band of brothers were screwing their way through the ship.

The Tasmanian never knew who'd be brought back to his shared cabin — 'One lot when I fall asleep, they've all changed by the time I wake up.'

Muffled, chinking parties were held on deck round the swimming pool after the close of the bar, and appropriate ship's personnel attended in case people rolled overboard. I really don't know how the Entertainments Officer stood up to it, but to their everlasting credit the crew stayed on their feet.

The manhandled shape the girls were in was fully revealed by bikinis — and life-boat drill, to which they reeled rather late. Innocent I might be, but my shape was greatly altered: my life-jacket was done up so tightly I thought I'd had a mastectomy.

We were cruising on dark, foam-dappled water, past a succession of broccoli islands – improbably viridian burgeoning out of the blue. Flying fish skimmed through the wave tops and the clouds made wallpaper patterns for the supreme egoist.

'If you've got to go overboard,' I drooled to a fellow-passenger, 'this is the place to go!'

'If you've got to go overboard—' (That was the First Officer.) 'Remember, keep your shoes on.'

'Wha—'

He frowned at me, for silence. 'We recommend shoes with closed toes. We do not recommend sandals. I would also suggest that you pray.'

'*Wha—*'

'*Loudly*, Madam. Sharks.' The frown wriggled around and became orientally philosophic. 'Australians say women and children first to dull the sharks' appetite.'

There was a whipping of wind against canvas. A bemused-looking Australian found the whistle in his life-jacket and blew it to see if it worked.

'*Pray*?' I screamed at the Officer, when we'd all uncovered our ears. 'Do the sharks only eat the agnostics?' It was about that time he got huffy, and tightened my laces again.

So long as we didn't pray for a repeat of one of the miracles; if anyone walked on the water, they'd trip themselves up on the fins.

Between sittings, examining myself anxiously in the cabin, I wondered whether my poor breasts would ever perk up and come out. In addition to being flattened, they were probably scared of the sharks.

And they weren't encouraged by Rock Eyes. She came back clenching an orange and said, 'That neckline's not very flattering!'

I knew better now than to argue; mind you, the clothes-hangers made quite a noise.

'And oh my God the food tonight! That meat was just swimming in grease. I had to leave half of it – how those men could eat it . . . Well, I just live for my roll.'

I disappeared into a jumper.

'And the dessert! If they call that chocolate—' She hooted. I could hear her, even deadened by wool. They could use her, if there was a fog. 'And those men were wolfing it down! I left them to it, I brought back some fruit.' Another hoot. 'An orange they call it! You ought to see mine at home — four times this size!'

She squeezed the defenceless orange, and stared candidly at my cowering front. 'D'you have a roll?'

'N—'

'Thought so! Dieting — you're much too thin!'

I'd have burst into tears if it wouldn't have seemed too touchy, and rushed to the bar for a quick snifter of tea. Perhaps my concave chest might respond to the dairy content? Perhaps I'd see an uncritical face — ah, that was a thought, yes, Hester . . . She might be able to suggest something or two. If I could persuade my breasts to part with my shoulder blades . . .

Hester saw me coming, with my purse already open, and flinched. 'Not more tea, not at half-past seven, I just can't bear it!' She went away and bought me a Horse's Neck.

Brandy and ginger ale had no effect on my bustline, but they anaesthetised my throat wonderfully, and after a couple I stopped worrying, so they were good for my morale. Classifying them legitimately as medicine, I poured the iced concoction over my scar tissue day after dry, air-conditioned day. So long as I watched the buggers on that boat, I felt I was sticking to sealed orders quite firmly enough.

It wasn't as if I had to sit watching the buggers alone.

CHAPTER SEVEN

The Purser watched them smoothly. He wore whites so blindingly white you couldn't see what he was doing and everything about him, including his hair, had been ironed.

Rock Eyes watched them with grim suspicion. She snapped that they stayed up all night and sounded envious.

The poor man from Tasmania did more than merely watch them. He tried to stay up with them, and one night after a film show he collapsed heavily on my shoulder, an interesting and apparently post mortem *eau de nil.*

Hester and I put our glasses on and scrutinised them keenly. We set up a base near the ping-pong and when we weren't watching and talking we were reading each other's books. I was unnerved by the speed with which she got through my light contribution, but then I bumped into the shaken astronomer. He'd lent her a book after dinner and had it returned, read, the following morning. The book was a dog-eared copy of a novel by John le Carré and it was *very* dog-eared because it had taken him three weeks to read.

Watching, I turned over pages and adjusted my wriggling towel. Having collected a pink front during the first few days on the Equator, I spent much of my time with my chest in the shade making efforts to get a matched back. Hester was sympathetic to my crab-like scuttlings. She had the colour that speaks of lifelong, ceaseless travel in hot countries. Unlikely to burn and uninterested in tanning, she gyrated her chair obligingly as I pursued squares of sun round the deck. Her long fingers, firm on *The Naked Civil Servant*, were wound about with rings.

'What's that one?' I asked lazily.

'An elephant saddle. Look—' She took the silver ring off and showed me. 'Interesting workmanship, see that? It comes from China.'

'You've been to—'

'No. Like to, though, one day. An American gave it to me in Egypt.'

Everything about her had a provenance and a family tree. Her blouses, her skirts, her hairpins, all came from some foreign place by some strange, circuitous route. 'Was this India?' she'd frown, grasping a handful of cotton. 'Or could it have been Burma? Oh, dear . . .' A great sigh, as flying fish skipped through the sparkle. 'Does it seem awfully stupid to be in love at my age?'

'I think it gets worse the older you get.' Vengefully I cracked the spine of a paperback. 'More painful, more agonising.'

'Oh . . . Yes, agony.'

'Like being cut open. Look at that!' I waggled *Vets in the Belfry* at the indigo skyline. 'I ought to be having a wonderful time! The ship's comfortable, the food's lovely, the weather's perfect — the only fly in the ointment's Rock Eyes. We're going to Australia and I've never been out of Europe before — and where do I want to be? London. God help me, Oxford Circus. I'm missing him so much I'm going *crazy*.'

'I know, I'm missing mine too.' Hester played with an earring. 'Isn't it *marvellous*?'

I did strange things to *Vets in the Belfry*. 'My throat's dry,' I announced. 'I'm—'

'Going to have some tea? No!' The only trouble with Hester was, she'd never grown up.

I flounced off to the refuelling station. When I inhaled my tea now, it didn't cost nearly so much. The buggers bought it for me, because they bought drinks for everyone and I wouldn't drink alcohol. Sometimes I found myself in the interesting position of having six cups of tea lined up and cooling along the bar. This was being a good girl and sticking to my sealed orders: 'I've seen you after two glasses—' So I drank tea with the buggers. Horse's Necks were drunk assiduously with Hester. whom I was unlikely to fancy even in the throbbing heat.

In order to assuage my scar tissue, not be poisoned by tannin and still follow orders, I dragged Hester to sit beside me at dances, where we peered myopically at the masses and laid bets on who very shortly would be doing what to whom.

There was a Captain's table by the dance floor as well as when dining, and there I was invited to sit, separated by a discreet caste system from the rest of the herd. If I in my turn invited Hester I could at least ease the cut-off with brandy. And there was someone with whom to discuss the rest of the herd: the women danced if they enjoyed it and the men danced if they couldn't get hold of the women any other way.

None of what I had been watching fell into this category. None of them were desperate, so they stayed in the bar and talked amongst themselves:-

'It's my round.'

'No it bloody isn't.'

'Yes it bloody is!'

'NO IT BLOODY ISN'T!'

Crash huff wallop *thump*.

The desperate ones were of uncertain age, rather short and narrow as to the trouser and wide as to the waist, and they came and asked me to do impossible things, like the fox-trot. I made Hester's year for her by accepting one of these challenges and being used like a motor mower to cut down the other dancers.

'I knew it!' she shrieked gleefully, rattling her ice-cubes. 'I knew he'd be like that! My dear, any man who shows that much sock . . .'

As the days passed and the girls fell by the wayside, more men attended the dances — though some of them reached a compromise by dancing in the bar. I became more popular through lack of competition: there'd been a decrease in numbers for which the buggers' libidos could not be held entirely to blame.

We were into the Indian Ocean, beyond the shelter of the islands, and in this world of upside-down seasons we were approaching Australian late autumn while England dripped in its late spring. The weather was slate grey and windy, and even force four felt considerable in our modest, compact little ship.

With the Hite Report pressed to their foreheads, the girls as one took to their bunks. The ship's doctor was sick saying 'Better?', the hairdresser was sick over perms, passengers watched their soup, hypnotised, and then rushed from the dining saloon.

'You awri'?' asked my little steward, patting me. 'You awri', Miss? You not si'?'

'No, thank you, I'm not,' I said. And amazingly wasn't. Between me and my stomach, I don't know which was the most surprised.

I bounced along companionways, lurched through exercises, staggered up to the buffet and skidded back down to my table with my plate cracking under the food. I had built-in stabilisers: a couple of gallons of tea.

'Oooruh!' groaned Hester. 'I'm going to lie down with a drink.'

'They say,' a young girl whimpered at the dinner table, 'it helps you to eat — ooooh!' And she wobbled away in a hurry, her pale forehead beaded with sweat.

Alarmed by the acute misery surging everywhere about me, I gave people travel-sickness pills which they instantly threw back up. The ship ploughed on its way and the only passengers ambulant were me and the kids and the buggers — and those sturdy girls not covered by basins and the Hite Report. My stock had never been higher, and I danced every night to a rhythm band that was sick

NEXT DANCE
DRUMMERS
EXCUSE ME

and sounded it. The dancers took no notice; we just enjoyed ourselves. We slid down the glassy floor into the drums and skated out into the tables, amidst warwhoops and feminine shrieks. I was held up by healthy young men who needed both hands to fasten their trousers, and after a soft, slow number in a swell their condition became critical. When the band were heaving too regularly to play anything but soft, slow numbers, the bruises started off by the tables crept all the way up to my neck.

Of course there were other, less violent amusements. Film shows — and my glass gathered speed as it slipped away from me, across the beam of light and under the chairs. When I drank tea I had to hold on to the bar counter, and helpful men held my bottom on to the bar stool for me. I thought it was very kind of them; a camaraderie had developed amongst those with sea-legs.

The amusements could also be formal. The Captain gave cocktail parties, beautifully catered, in his own quarters, and his pictures swung tipsily through wide arcs on the walls. The cocktail parties were more than formal: select. One consisted of him and the Purser, and the catering.

Feeling I should take the chance to see the bridge by daylight, I joined a tough party and was shown *where we were* and *how they knew*. The only unfortunate result of an otherwise happy occasion was that somewhere or other I collected a patch of varnish-stripper on my jacket and had to skitter down to the cabin to wash it off. I'd timed my visit badly, no bell had yet chimed and Rock Eyes was supine on her bunk.

Rock Eyes had taken speedily to the horizontal at the first suggestion of a three-inch wave, and there she had stayed while I brought her rounds of toast. She was older than me, she did sometimes say the right thing (into the mirror, slapping on powder: 'You old dink!') and I was shamed into real solicitude. The solicitude was weakened when I brought her toast tenderly wrapped in a napkin and she said, 'You look pale. I just hope you don't get sick, I don't want to nurse you. And suppose I starved to death?' This seemed a pleasant but remote possibility, considering the alacrity with which she recovered for lunch. She also recovered for dinner — a portrait of a lady who lived for a roll. Betweenwhiles she lay sleeping, and since she slept all day she was less deeply asleep by night. Her fitful, wakeful dozing had presented sufficient hazards, but now there was the awful silence since the air-conditioning had been switched off. This combination of factors had put the block on my homework, and I was becoming jumpy and exceedingly tight of lip.

Deprivation must have addled my aching brain-pan, otherwise why return to the cabin at such an ill-timed juncture?

'You're not sick, are you?'

'No, I—'

'That's good.' She watched my frantic scrabblings with the stained jacket, her eyes reverted to their original slits. The sea was choppy and flung me about the ablutions, till I steadied myself by catching hold of a passing coat-hook. With one hand I clawed at the sticky varnish-stripper. Oh, for a nail-brush — I'd have to make do with my nails . . .

Out of the corner of my ear I heard Rock Eyes turn over.

The jacket leapt in the water, with muscles like Action Man. Scratch, scratch — when I think what these nails are used for. Varnish-stripper — that they should come to this. The ship rolled and I lost touch with the coat-hook. I caught hold of a door handle instead and the door flung itself open. I caught hold of a basin and it slithered through my fingers. I caught hold of a towel-rail and a wall and a bright tooth-mug . . .

'Alyda!' came an icy hiss. 'Were you using my toothbrush?'

Rock Eyes' toothbrush was the type that is wonderful for dentures. It needed to be, and the sight of its slim lines gave me the creeps. I'm affected that way by common images of things to come. One day I'll need a wig and hormone replacement, and a seeing-eye dog and some dental fixative. One day I will also need a coffin, but in the meantime I'd rather not be reminded that I started decaying the moment I was born.

The thought of touching Rock Eyes' special toothbrush sent vipers wriggling up and down my spine.

'I grabbed hold of – '

'What were you doing there? Were you using it?'

'*Using* it?'

'You were scraping at your jacket – what were you scraping at it with just now?'

'My fingernails!'

'Not my toothbrush?'

'No, not your toothbrush!'

Rock Eyes narrowed her lips and they disappeared. 'Alyda, you're sure you're telling me the truth now?'

'I WAS NOT USING YOUR – '

'All right.' It plainly wasn't. 'If you say you're sure . . .'

Silent, I hung my jacket up to drip-dry. My heart was pounding in my ears with the lust for murder, and my fingers on the hanger were white with strain.

Half-way to the lounge, I remembered a favourite book that I'd forgotten, and lurched back to the cabin through the middle of the heaving ship. The door fell open to reveal a brilliant tableau: Rock Eyes, vertical, in pink silk slip and curlers, under the light examining her toothbrush. She glinted at me. Perry Mason. 'This toothbrush is damp!'

'This *cabin* is damp! *I* am damp!' (And how, with no occupational therapy.) 'When the ship rolled it threw me around – everything I touched is damp! Here, look at the walls! That cockroach is soaking wet!'

It was no good protesting. Rock Eyes did not believe me. She cut down on verbiage, hid her dentifrice and didn't see me. If I'd realised it was that easy, I'd have danced on her toothbrush days before. And to think of the hours I'd wasted, directing cockroaches towards her bunk.

Unfortunately, the trip was nearly over. The ship settled its shoulders and steadied, and more people put their feet on the floor of their cabins, heartened by the prospect of foreseeable landfall. In this agreeable calm I sat in the bar catching up on my letters. The afternoon was perfect. And then my cup and saucer started rattling . . .

'Cullents,' said the barman. 'Don't wully, Miss. You li' choose a ta'?' He was washing glasses that jingled disconcertingly when he set them aside to drain.

Swaying in thought, I chose a tape cassette from the large box beside the player and exited smartly, before the amplified boom I'd left behind could reach to me out of the bar. Let those go deaf early who still had mothers-in-law. Troublesome ears I could do without – I had enough trouble already, with my abused packer's back. Not that it had complained to me lately; it hadn't been aching for days. What a relief after the drama! And I'd thought at the time that I'd never make London Airport. Well, here I was, only a day away from Fremantle, one of the few who hadn't been sick and physically as sound as a bell. My lungs had even survived the steward's anti-cockroach spray. *I* could tolerate it almost as well as the cockroaches. From *their* reaction to it, you'd have thought it was Aramis.

And my dancing was improving. Of course it was all a question of having natural balance.

I had one sole on the second step when the whole of the boat turned sideways, my sandals skipped on the carpet and I fell head-over-heels down three flights.

We were due to sight land around midnight. We'd be docking tomorrow, sometime in the afternoon.

I lay motionless in the corridor, waiting and hoping to breathe. I watched my ribs but nothing happened. Where had I acquired this unerring instinct for last-minute catastrophe? Before leaving, paralysis; before arriving, death.

The ship effortlessly flipped me over, as though it were turning a piece of fried haddock in a hot pan. The movement wasn't quite what I'd have asked, but at least it started a bit of air going in and out. Very gradually, very nervously, I gathered my limbs together. They seemed to be connected, however tenuously, to my hulk. I tried moving them, very gently. They were unenthusiastic. I felt like a puppeteer with half the strings off her marionette.

Knee by knee, elbow by elbow, one wall at a time I hoisted myself to my feet. It was a terrible moment when I realised I'd have to get back down for my writing pad. But somehow I managed it, and somehow, in stages (the gift shop, the hairdressing salon) I winced my way to my bunk. I *could* move – I'd proved it. There was only one problem: pain.

'Ah!' said Hester wisely, when I'd grown rather bored with the rack and had dragged myself up to the lounge. 'Ah! I say, that bruise is going to be *gorgeous*! Now, if you'd been *drunk* at the time you wouldn't have felt a *thing*.'

'But I'm not supposed to get drunk! Ooooh!' (I'd bounced in my chair and hit on a hurt.)

'My dear, I must say you're carrying this business far too far. There's no need to get completely pie-eyed. You could have a *couple* of drinks – what harm would that do?'

'None – ouch! – if you stay with me.'

'But you're perfectly all right when you're with me and you have more than two drinks!'

'Hester, that's just because you *are* with me. I get silly with gentlemen, Hester. I lose all my sense of proportion, and I start to kiss them, and –'

'And?'

'And I start to kiss them.' I rubbed my knees miserably. 'And –'

'Yes, you said that. And they object to this, do they?'

'No, but my husband used to.'

'But you told me you're no longer married!'

'That's right, I'm sort of – occupied.'

'And *he* objects to this, does he?'

'When it isn't directed at him.'

Hester did things with her ice-cubes.

'It really is awful, Hester – I just wrap myself round everybody!' I wrapped myself round my tender portions. 'And with no discrimination – Messalina on a wine-gum! I'd find something to love about Hitler. Oooo-oow!'

'*Now* what's the matter?'

'He could have won the war with these chairs.'

'But Hitler isn't here, dear. I don't think you need worry. Enough gin and even I might find *him* fascinating, but we've only got these extra*ord*inary young men.'

'Yes, but–'

'You've had a shock and you need brandy – think, if you'd been drunk you would have *floated* down those stairs. Come on, brandy's *good* for you, my goodness. That and a nice lie-down . . . Quite cured me of being sea-sick, I intend to dance this evening and I don't care if the ship stands on its head.'

Hester wasn't the only one feeling eager, to judge by the revellers being thrown around the lounge. She waved her glass at me. 'And you'd better dance as well, if you don't want rigor mortis. Worst thing that could happen is for you to stiffen up. We can always sit with Howard as a last resort against the fox-trot.'

Howard was the astronomer, a kind man who'd taken us out to see constellations upside-down. Neither of us were of the opinion that he was interested in dancing, and if we were approached by short trousers bent on the chassis we could always say that we were sitting one out with him.

So that night I sat, obediently pouring in brandy, with one hand holding me steady and one eye on the astronomer. It was not part of his brief to protect me from the buggers, and I was crossing my bruises that he wouldn't exceed his duty. Viewed through a prism of alcohol and night starvation, the buggers were beginning to look extremely attractive to me. One of them loomed benevolently and jerked his head at the dance-floor, but when I unfolded on to my feet it turned out he'd been jerking at Hester.

Hester did quite well, really. Yes. Quite well, considering. What with dancing *every single* dance and being bought all those glasses of champagne. 'I had no idea!' she panted, when I had been molested alongside her. 'I didn't know they'd brought the Charleston back. None – whoops! Oh, my goodness! Stop it, you're young enough to be my nephew! What *do* they do with their hands?'

'Let's just hope they wash them first.' I was being muttered at by my partner; despite being totally inaudible, he was managing to make his presence felt.

'Alida!' A shriek, that must be Hester. 'Should he really have his hands on your behind?'

'Ssssh, don't let him hear you, for God's sake! He'll try to put them where they were before!'

At one point I caught a glimpse of the astronomer. He was being firmly danced with by a very well-covered Maori, his ears had gone flat against his head and *she* was leading *him*.

It was all very athletic and noisy, and amorous and drunken. It was, I suppose, a typical last night at sea. But I had no way of knowing. The longest sea trip I'd ever made had been on a cross-Channel ferry, and then my only attachment had been to the man who held my head while I threw up.

On the chill, windswept deck in the early hours of the morning, with the lights of Geraldtown shimmering and winking from the dark, invisible coastline of Western Australia, I suddenly felt very nervous at the thought of stepping on land. The buggers on board ship (and at that moment one particular bugger) might be as reliable as rhinos, but at least they were buggers I knew.

'Two months? You're crazy!'

'Yes I am, probably.'

'You don't mean he expects—'

'Oh, yes he does. Besides, you must be tired. Don't you think you should lie down?'

'Waddayathink I'm asking?'

'I meant on your own! For the past six days you and a few friends of yours have been helping this ship through the water. Relax, we're nearly there now. You can unpack your double surfboard.'

'But *two months* for Chrissake!'

'Believe me, I'm peculiar. Don't worry about me.'

Back home in London, in the midst of the storm of packing, with the back of my throat still looking like an exceptionally vivid trifle, I had broken down, wailing, at the enormity of it all. I couldn't do it, I simply couldn't, I couldn't cope with everything and be ready to leave in a week. And my bloke had been very cool and calm and told me not to worry. I'd sat there, tearful, waiting for him to take over. 'Don't worry,' he'd said kindly. 'It'll be awful for me — your being away like that — but don't you worry about me.'

'You'd better not waste any more time,' I said. 'Everyone else is getting fixed up.'

'That's OK. I like a good story. I still think you're shooting a line. Sweetheart, no one's worth it.'

'That's right, love. Goodnight.'

And so I lay listening to Rock Eyes' breath and the cockroaches. And the cabin creaking. And my rattled thoughts. And in the morning I got a cable that said how much he was thinking of me, and I was very glad I'd watched the buggers on that boat.

CHAPTER EIGHT

'You met *what* on the boat?'

'A male prostitute.'

'You mean a prostitute for fellers?'

'No, a prostitute for women.'

'That's the brewery,' said Stephen, from the darkness of the back seat.

'Jesus *Christ*! And where d'yer say he came from? Can't have been Perth — Sydney?'

'Wait a minute . . .' I scrabbled around in my handbag. 'He gave me his address . . .'

Stephen and Chas looked at each other in the rear-view mirror.

'Here we are — Brisbane.'

'*Brisbane? BRISBANE?* You have got to be kidding!'

'No, I don't think so. Look, he gave me his telephone number — is it really true we'll only be there a couple of days?'

'Why?' said Stephen.

'Well, there were some friends of mine in London who said "Brisbane — that's the pits". So I was pleased it was only two days. I must have misunderstood them, I never realised they meant pits of depravity. Is Brisbane like Copenhagen — lots of male prostitutes?'

The car swerved erratically. Stephen said 'That's the brewery' and Chas let out a shriek: 'Those banana benders! They don't even have mixed bathing! Jesus Christ, Alida, they've never got round to having *female* prostitutes!'

'Perhaps that's why he made enough to go to Europe for three years.'

'Three years?' repeated Stephen. He'd been looking tired, but now he looked tired and thoughtful.

'Yes. Three whole years without working, but he worked his arse off before. He told me he made deep researches into women and female orgasm, and he earned enough for a water bed and a Bang and Olofsson Beosystem *and* a Norton Commando, but he didn't like having no girl friends because he had no energy — and when he did have the energy he always had to protect it — so he sold his car and his apartment and went to Europe for a rest.'

'Was he very good-looking?' Stephen was patting his hair flat in the flickering rear-view mirror.

'He had personality.'

Chas was very pale, or it may have been the illuminations. First he said 'That's the brewery' and then he said 'Jesus Christ.'

'I thought he was fascinating. I'd like to interview him — don't you think going to see him would make a good interview?'

Stephen and Chas looked at each other in the mirror, eloquently.

'I brought my tape recorder.'

Chas got stuck in 'Park' for a minute and then said 'He'll be glad of that.'

'He said he'd devoted *ages* to studying female orgasm — there are all these married women who've never had one in their life.'

'I can believe it, in Brisbane.'

'Yes, he said they were crying out. Their husbands go away on business — he told me one of them told *him* she thought her right hand would fall off.'

Stephen started coughing and Chas pointed out the brewery.

'He started out with an escort service.'

Stephen tapped me on the shoulder and asked me what

I thought of the lights.

They had waited for me for hours, in a bleak terminal in the rain, and I had begun to fear that there'd be no one waiting to meet me, it was taking so long to disembark.

Hester and I had lost sight of each other, the astronomer had vanished, and for a while I'd been stranded with Rock Eyes, whose glaciers knew no bounds. She'd put her wig on over her curlers, to look grand for disembarkation, and in the squally weather I'd have been glad of a wig myself. But one of the buggers had dragged us on deck to view approaching Australia, and had howled through the wind and sleet 'This'll sort out who's wearing the wigs!' Rock Eyes had pounced on him, squealing 'What d'you mean by that?' and when he had reeled around, burbling his innocence, she had thrown a disbelieving, pure caracara glance at me. *I* had betrayed her (how else would he have guessed it?) and might also betray her in Woollongong — fellow-occupant of her cabin and witness to her manoeuvrings with shiny nylon and elastic net.

For the second time, and finally, she sent me to Coventry.

Shortly prior to our arrival, there had been a brief and unwelcome break in my sentence, because she had to ask *someone* whether she should declare her plant. She had to ask fairly often. I was lost in packing and a cable-pink reverie. In fact, all that morning, I had a cable-pink view of the world.

The little steward and I had emotionally patted each other — how hard he'd tried to make the cabin nicer for me. Spraying it till his can ran out, carefully wiping off tear-stains and making 'Stand up to her!' faces behind the wall-to-wall bulk of Rock Eyes.

After the fond farewells I'd pulled myself together and, mindful of cockroaches, I'd furiously shaken my scanties as I removed them from the cupboards and drawers and laid them in my cases. Rock Eyes had sniffed like a dredger: 'That's a good hotel you're going to – better unpack on a sheet.'

'But I don't think –'

'If they knew what *you* were bringing in, they wouldn't serve you a tea!' She laughed, which was unpleasant. She was *very* careful with her toothbrush of late, and her dentures had not been improved.

'From what *I've* heard of Australia,' I shrilled (even a slow-worm can turn) 'cockroaches are the *last* thing you've got to worry about! They were telling me only last night, you've got the most terrible spiders – great, huge, horrible things, as big as tarantulas!'

'Huh!' Her poppet-beads shuddered. 'Only way they'll hurt you is if they trip you up.'

'And what about the little red ones?'

'Oh, yeah. Well, those are fatal.' Woollongong Rock at last looked worried. 'I just wish I knew whether I should declare my plant.'

I wrung a pair of my knickers. Luckily at that moment they were uninhabited.

For over a week now Rock Eyes' plant had shared our cabin – a tender, inoffensive shoot she'd kidnapped somewhere in Europe. Because of the threat of alien contagion, it hadn't been allowed to retain a trace of foreign earth. Listlessly it declined in a bed of wet Australian cotton-wool. Its presence was so undemanding that it only rarely impinged on my consciousness. Sufficient unto my days the evil of the ineradicable eight-legged clatter, and the unblinking scrutiny to which I'd been subjected before *l'affaire* toothbrush.

Sometimes I'd noticed it, before I forgot it, alone and palely loitering beside the uncurtained porthole. Rock Eyes didn't talk to it as my friends talk to their plants, but she picked it up and scowled at it, as though it had wet its nappy. At times like that, I sent it waves of sympathy – if I'd been a little bit smaller, I had the feeling Wollongong Rock would have done that to me.

'If I tell them about it they'll take it away because of

the fruit fly and if I *don't* tell them about it I'll be breaking the law.'

I went on grimly shaking.

'Perhaps I *won't* tell them about it. I've brought it all this way – '

There was a knock at the door: our steward, with the iced water.

When he'd gone, Wollongong Rock sat fingering her cotton-wool. 'They tip them off,' she niggled.

Startled, I looked at her. At every opportunity, Rock Eyes refused to tip.

'They act as informants!' Her lips had disappeared again, and she was taut around the nose. 'If I don't declare it, *he*'ll tell them about my plant.'

'Oh, for goodness' sake! Don't you think you're being – '

'You don't know about Orientals. And they stick together.'

'Do you mean the Customs Men are going to be oriental?'

'What d'yer mean by that?' Wollongong Rock was outraged. 'We don't have Orientals! They can try paddling down but they'll never penetrate us! What newspapers have you been reading? You've been reading those papers in England! Refugees from Vietnam – '

'Nothing! I swear to – '

'Our Australian Customs are all Australian!'

This, in the event, meant that Australian Customs were the slowest in the world.

Mind you, they were affable.

Very affably, ten at a time, we were leaked off the sodden deck and into the terminal. And there dangerous immigrants were affably taken apart. Between each minuscule intake, the Customs Men flipped through their clip-boards and the porters had a smoke.

Three hours after docking I was three yards nearer the gangplank. Quietly but with drama, I began to cry.

As far as I knew, I was being met by the local Australian distributor. Neither of us had the slightest idea what the other looked like. He had been given the exact time of the liner's arrival and by now, I was certain, he'd have decamped with an Eskie of beer. What was I going to do, and what would happen to me?

None of the faces around me was even faintly familiar. This was the first time I'd seen them – they must have been at different sittings, and on different, submarine decks.

The buggers had split like the Red Sea, but had not united again. Some had remained in the bowels, laying anything that was recumbent and drinking from laid-in supplies. The rest had inserted themselves magically into the first few issues from the boat. They weren't visible round the strange faces, but they were so loud I could hear.

Of Hester, and the astronomer, and even Rock Eyes there was no sign.

Landfall in Australia. The local man would have given up and gone to his local hours ago. The city itself must be miles away from this dump (and the dockside looked a dump, cranes and cars through the lashing rain, night falling early, an appallingly derelict cruiser flying the American flag, to which a lone bugger had pointed and yelled 'The Australian Navy!').

Rain streamed down my tear-streaked face, washed out my salty hair-do and trickled remorselessly into the neck of my coat.

'Coats!' Hester had chortled. 'My dear, you just won't need them! I've never been that cold – I haven't worn one in Australia yet!'

It was as well that, standing weeping and dripping on the windswept deck, I had no idea that ahead of me lay the coldest Australian winter for eighty years.

'All right!' called a sodden official, thumbing us down the gangplank and into the terminal.

And I squelched towards the concrete and lights, running down somebody's child. Supposing there weren't any taxis? Surely there had to be taxis! And how about

B
BBBBB

finding a porter – I couldn't see any of those . . .

OhmyGod. Suddenly, there in the terminal, I realised something I should have realised a long time before. I wasn't wearing my contact lenses! And my glasses were God knew where in the sordid mess of my bulging hand-luggage.

The salt wind had spat in my eyes and made them too sore for lenses. Hours ago, as I'd stood waiting, taking them out had seemed a bright idea.

Oh, *Christ*, even if the local man was still loyally waiting, and *holding up a notice*, I wouldn't be able to see it! Putting my lenses back in involved water and wetting solution . . . And to think, Hester's queue might have been near me all this time! No wonder I hadn't been able to recognise any of those faces!

I threw myself, blubbering, into the arms of a porter. He was very nice to me, once I'd blown my nose.

My cases, he told me politely, when he'd asked me my surname, would be in the section over there, under the big letter 'B'. Could I see them, and which were they? It threw him off balance slightly when I had to tell him I couldn't see the section, let alone the letter 'B'.

He led me over to the section, and said 'Are these your cases?' and I put my face close to the handles and was able to tell him 'Yes'.

We trundled briskly towards the Customs. Actually he was doing the trundling, but I was afraid to lose him so I trotted briskly behind. When he stopped trundling, I ran into him, and he said 'Does anyone here know you?' He was gazing, intently, so I screwed up my eyes and peered. At the barrier, two faint forms were leaping about and waving. *Two* forms? I swallowed. I had short-sight – wasn't that enough? Not the big one – double vision. I screwed up my eyes more tightly.

Surely . . . but it couldn't be. One of the forms looked faintly – very faintly – familiar. It looked (but it couldn't be) like my publisher's chap, the one I was supposed to meet in Perth, eventually. Eventually. Not now. He was supposed to be in Hong Kong.

The forms went on leaping, and pointing, and waving. The porter stared at them, and me, and said 'Which of them's your hubby?' and I said 'Neither, thank God!' I was having another cry.

Even the all-Australian Customs Man was nice. He smiled. He *smiled* at me, and welcomed me to Australia, and said he hoped I'd have a good time, and didn't open my luggage. And the porter was *surprised* when I gave him a tip.

And then there they were, at the barrier — both of them. A stocky, muscular, suntanned man and a rather pale, jet-lagged Stephen, with the inside of his head still in Hong Kong.

Stephen peeled me off and said 'This is Chas' and Chas said 'Of course I wudda waited!'

'But I thought you would have gone home hours ago!'

'If I'd bin here on my own I'd 'a held up one of the books and shouted out "Who's got thrush?"'

They carried everything for me, the cases, the packets, the hand-luggage, and bundled me into the warm car, and drove me over the sweeping, beautiful, glittering freeway into Perth, and said 'That's the brewery.'

CHAPTER NINE

'But they're so awfully pretty!'

Chas perspired and said 'Don't worry. Don't worry,' and Stephen boggled from behind his briefcase, mute.

'They make me look like Quasimodo!'

Chas hearteningly gripped my elbow and said 'Did yer have to do yer own hair?'

'Aaawwooohh!'

Stephen's ears twitched in my direction and Chas said 'Christ, what I'd do fer a beer.'

'I thought someone *professional* would put on my make-up!'

Chas said 'I just wish yer'd asked my daughter — she'da come and done yer hair.'

'For God's sake, Chas, if it's all that bad at least I can comb it — I can't run a comb through my face! I thought there'd be special make-up for television — I've left all my usual stuff off. I'm lucky I've got eyes! I wouldn't have those if it weren't for Reception! I didn't want to give the man behind the desk a heart attack. My God, Chas, I put on blusher to take in the milk! I can't go on TV without any make-up! Chas, stop sweating like that — WHAT AM I GOING TO DO?'

One of the pretty girls shrugged. From the back it was interesting. From the side it was devastating. From the front it could have competed for effect with the Neutron bomb.

'What will I do without make-up?'

Chas mopped at himself with a hankie and said 'How

high can yer hold up the books?'

The girls had arrived a quarter of an hour after we had, late and unrepentant, in the impersonal white make-up room. At least their arrival confirmed that we were waiting in the right place. The spartan room contained not a trace of indigent make-up, nor a make-up artist; just light bulbs, mirrors and dentists' chairs. It looked like the set for the scene where they torture the spy.

Our gruesome group was in a corner, in a huddle, giving the impression that we did this all the time. Chas was perspiring so much he might well have had swamp fever, Stephen was smoking his fingers and I was searching my handbag in hopes of striking some Kohl.

Chas had just emitted a fresh burst of encouragement: 'This'll be easy compared ter termorrer' and 'Yer didn't ferget the titles' when the young ladies came in.

We stared at them, riveted, and they sauntered up to the mirrors and critically stared at themselves. Then they unpacked a portable Max Factor outlet. This would have been less galling to me if either of them had needed it. They were, before they licked their lips or spat on mascara, the two most breathtakingly pretty girls that I had ever seen. I listened rapt to their conversation. Somewhere on their shapely persons, each of them must have secreted a powerful megaphone.

'Chris cut my fringe last Thursday.'

'Yeah, I saw. It's beaut.'

'I could tie it back before.'

'Yeah, I saw. Beaut.'

'I still wish he hadn't done it.'

'Yeah. But it's beaut.'

This was the first, but not the last, time I heard this strange word. On the boat I had learned other Australian terms of approbation. The only two repeatable were 'Fuckin' marvellous' and 'bloody great'. I had come to imagine the use of 'beaut' was an ugly rumour, spread by British migrants when they found out they'd have to work. Hell hath no fury like a Briton defending his tea-break, and many a country has fallen under the British cultural back-lash.

'Oh — you got that frosted mauve eyeshadow.'

'Yeah. Isn't it beaut?'

We gazed at them in awe. One of them had such a face she really *must* have been called Pansy, but she didn't seem to be long for this world because of the state of her fringe. The other had been breast-fed on double cream and bananas, but whenever she opened her head somewhere a foghorn went 'Beaut!'

This paralysing pair were to be on the programme modelling glasses. The designer would rest his frames on their camellia faces, and the world would rush out to buy his frames so *they* could look like that.

'Hey — have you tried this new lash-fixative? It's hypo-allergenic.'

'Yeah, I've tried it. Beaut.'

By modelling alone, they could have sold amputation to an athlete. Without anaesthesia. Provided they kept their mouths shut.

'Yeah, I like your hair that way. Beaut.'

Pansy shrugged.

A vice gripped my elbow, Chas' voice was hoarse: 'Jesus *Christ*!'

'Not my hair again! What's the matter?'

'Didyer see the size of her nipples?'

'NO!'

'Didn'yer put yer lenses in?'

I was making a noise like a coffee percolator. If no make-up appeared within the next five minutes, I would go over and steal the opposition's base coat.

'Stephen. Stephen! How about those nipples?' But Stephen was off in a world all his own: one in which, undoubtedly, Pansy's nipples loomed large. 'Didyer ever see anything like that? Stephen! Jesus *Christ*!'

By now I had also decided to steal Foghorn's frosted lip-glosser. There was absolutely no way of stealing a march on Pansy.

'Hey — have you got my eyelash curlers?'

'Yeah. Thanks a lot. Beaut.'

Foghorn also had a compact of brush-on face shaper . . . I began edging nearer to her box.

The dastardly act was circumvented by the presenter, a porcelain lady, who twitched when she saw me and trilled urgently 'Make-*up*!' How could anyone be so charming at that early hour of the morning? She was not only sweet and immaculately groomed, she'd actually read all my books. She'd be asking me this and that about them and Heavens was my husband really that bad and was that true, what I'd written about his hair? For the first time I suffered an uneasy tremor which had nothing whatsoever to do with my looks.

'Chas!' I hissed. 'Chas, have you got a copy?' I'd been divorced a year and the first book was written four years ago; I'd forgotten what I'd said my husband was like.

'His hair *really* came out that much?' asked the presenter.

'Well—' My sweaty fingers paused in the pages. 'I do remember I had to Hoover the sheets.'

I was sat in a chair and sponged over by a girl with a pony-tail, who worked layers of pancake deep down through my pores. 'I won't touch your eyes,' she said, as she drowned me in powder.

'Why not?' I choked.

'You've got enough on — d'you want to have 'em nailed shut?'

There was a nasty moment when Chas crept up behind me, and whispered 'Tell 'em about yer piles!' in my pancaked ear. The pony-tailed girl covered herself in powder. 'And remember yer've gotta say the name of the publishers, and if they ask tell 'em *we* distribute the books.'

'Chas!' I squeaked, rearing round in a cloud of beige Leichner. 'My mind's gone a blank — I can't remember a thing!'

Pause. He'd stopped breathing. No he hadn't — but his teeth were chattering. When he spoke, it was in a strange falsetto. 'Don't worry,' he stuttered. 'Don't worry.'

'I won't if you'll leave me alone!'

It was my first experience of Australian television. It was my first experience of *any* television. I took my contact lenses out; if I couldn't see them, I wouldn't be cowed. But suppose I tripped over a cable? Grittily, I put my contact lenses in again.

Now, what was she likely to ask me? Questions about my husband? (Oh, God.) Questions about my marriage? (Oh, *God*.) Questions about the books? I riffled madly. It was another life — *my* life, before the great divide. There was life before divorce, and I'd written three books to prove it.

Why?

I went on riffling, hoping to find an answer. When all that was happening to me, it hadn't seemed funny at all. It had only seemed funny when I wrote it down. Now I was reading it and I'd been right: it didn't seem funny. Not even being deflowered after my pile-job, by two nuns with a dildo.

'You all right?' asked Stephen. The query amounted to an eruption; ever since Pansy's nipples, he'd been sunk in thought.

'Yes,' I said, lying. My scar tissue clamoured for caffeine. I wouldn't have minded a Horse's Neck. But I wasn't going to get it. Back came the porcelain presenter, and I was led off to the studio and shown a nook and a white tweed couch.

'Oh, God,' said the presenter. 'Not this old thing again!' She studied herself in the monitor and arranged her skirt. She was satisfied. I studied myself in the monitor and couldn't arrange a thing. I wasn't satisfied, I was terrified. The red light was glowing, there wasn't time for surgery.

'And today we have . . .'

For the whole of the interview, I was conscious of a small screen showing what looked to me like a busty moose with a deep sun tan. She had some terrible mannerisms and appeared in brilliant colour in the corner of my eye.

The programme was taped in segments, and after the bit with me in I sat and waited with Chas and Stephen. I was to be a guest speaker on a panel dealing with viewers' queries, and our weightless comments were to form the end of the show. We watched the other interviews, and the current affairs slot, and the spectacular frames on Pansy and Foghorn. Between each segment we chatted. Translated, this meant that I chatted and Chas and Stephen considered Pansy's perky avoirdupois. It was a fairly long, contented programme, gentle and entertaining and very professional. It was even entertaining to take part in – apart from the horrifying glimpses of the busty moose in the monitor.

'We can get back to the hotel in time to see it on TV!' A prospect that had Chas excited. Obviously anything was better than having to see me live.

We walked back to the car, and the brilliant sunshine beat down on my pancake-coated pores. The sky had cleared, the rain had evaporated after my arrival in Australia and left hot dry days and chill sudden evenings – no twilight and instant nightfall about five pm. This morning Perth glinted, scrubbed and wholesome in dips and rises, comfortable shoulders of suburbs and parkland, a curve of towering commerce, a sweep of shimmering water and, within minutes, bush. Not bush with swagmen – bush hadn't turned out to mean that. Bush had turned out to mean country, fairly tidied up.

I paused by the car door, wind in my hair, getting my bearings. The light was so clear that I felt my eyes had been scrubbed. If only I had more time, if I was in one place longer, the space, the brightness, might cease to be a shock.

I'd scrambled ashore late on that rainy Saturday, been

driven to the hotel and shown into my hotel suite, and Chas had said 'Well, I read the books' when I blinked at the massive double bed. The suite was so large I got lost in the wardrobe – the entrance lobby was the smallest place and that was the size of my Wendy House.

When I'd found my way out we went down to the Grill Room and ate oysters the size of ping-pong balls and steaks like *Gone with the Wind.* Chas told me his life story, and I told him my life story, and neither of us listened, and I insisted on seeing the hotel's discothèque and while we were dancing I realised Stephen had gone to sleep.

Sunday I had slept late, lingering gluttonous over breakfast, and then Chas had spent the day showing Stephen and me round the city and driving us out to meet his horses. It was all so *clean*, so immaculate in the sunshine, so healthy and so spacious – bedazzled, I heard Chas say 'D'yer have the trots?'

'No, the steaks were lovely.'

'Horses, I mean! Horses!'

'Wuh – ah. No, I don't think so. We just have horse-racing.' All I knew about racing was the local betting shop.

'Wait'll yer see the trots. Yer'll love the trots, won't she, Stephen?'

Stephen had been concentrating on a girl in a mini-skirt. Girls in Australia were defiantly wearing them, which probably accounted for the wistful look in Stephen's eye.

'If you think so, then perhaps I'd –'

'Yeah, sure, I'll have to arrange it. Stephen loved the trots, didn't yer love the trots Stephen? The trots and the footie.'

'Oh, yeah. Loved 'em. That's right, Chas. Marvellous.' There was something about Stephen. Afterwards he took me in an unbreakable arm-lock. 'You do not like the trots! Understand, you do not like them!'

'No,' I said. 'Of course not! You're breaking my arm,

Stephen, please put it down!'

'The trots are the most *boring* — Don't you dare give Chas an opening! You do know I'd have to come too? And you were saying yes to him! I don't know how I didn't kill you.'

'Yes, Stephen. No, Stephen.'

We never did go to the trots.

But we did go to the horses (Chas' own special horses) and the kangaroo and the aviary. How we got to them, and by what route, I ceased to be certain. After the first few heart-attacks, I'd clutched my seat and closed my eyes. Now I realised why wearing seat-belts was compulsory. There had to be some way of keeping the passengers in the car.

Watching, sweating, someone veer straight across our bows and turn to the right after a left-hand signal, I asked whether it was very easy to get a driving licence in Australia. Chas tapped the roof of the car and said 'Knowin' the shape of the wheels helps.'

Tapping on the roofs of cars seemed to give driving Australians something to do with their hands.

He had transported us (me quivering) from the hotel forecourt, through the shining city and up to the chlorophyll King's Park, pointing out with whatever came handy Perth's ancient monuments. Ancient monuments were not the ladies with stiff hair and strange hemlines, they were any building more than fifty-five years old.

If you talk about anywhere and refer to its newness — a new city, a new country, a new continent — you're usually thinking of roughness, unpolished manners and edges, and everything being raw.

As we had drawn near to Fremantle, I had stared at the flat, grey coastline and whimpered to one of the buggers 'Doesn't it look uninhabited? Doesn't it look uncivilised? 'Doesn't it look uninteresting?' and Woollongong Rock had slavered '*Why*?' But the broken, rain-drenched illusion had given way to polished Perth, and Perth being new wasn't one bit like the newness of a Spanish ribbon development, where the hotels are half-constructed, where the scaffolding is odd-angled pit-props and the tourists fall down the earthworks and are never seen again.

Perth's novelty was the newness of unscathed sky-scrapers, of fresh-painted houses, of space and light and air and a reeling ribbon of freeway joining the homes to the city centre.

This kind of newness was one I'd never before encountered, but was to see again and again all over Australia. A smooth, un-dirty newness, like a window display of G-Plan. Little being dirty, and even less being old. And nothing that was old was dirty, because it was so thoroughly washed and preserved and admired and pointed out and boned up.

'Why're yer old buildin's fallin' down?' an Australian asked me. Unanswerable. 'We don't let ours fall down!'

And to try to explain the age of our commonplace old buildings was to try to explain the colour blue to a man who was born blind.

Yes, it was extraordinary to see a Town Hall that was built by convicts, and Chas gestured at the broad arrows slyly worked in its clock-tower's design. And the Barracks Archway, all that's left of the soldier settlers' headquarters, solitary and sturdy brickwork at the top of St George's Terrace. And the Treasury Building, and the sudden, occasional churches – but what was most extraordinary was how amazingly *unsullied* they all were.

From the vantage point of King's Park, Stephen and I looked out over the city, and took ill-considered snapshots, and clicked at trees and the Swan River and the tailored green. It was beautiful, beautiful – and hot and sunny yet winter – and to me, far from smutty London, incredibly alien.

Somehow the fact that everyone spoke my native language made the foreignness more disturbing still. People in England sneer about Australian accents, but the accents around me were far more readily intelligible than many I was used to hearing in London. Yet I felt as though I'd been landed on Mars by bugger-manned spaceship. Nowhere the disorder, nowhere the narrow chaos, nowhere the dust and the grime and the rush and the smell of the packed Underground. The *pavements* in St George's Terrace were wider than the one-way street near Oxford Circus where I lived. All the new buildings, all the neat houses, all the smart boats and the trim, prim, posh yachts . . . Even the air smelled deodorised, even the trees and the parklands had short haircuts. Perth was a city wearing its best bib and tucker. Only the swans dipping their beaks for fresh bread on the clean water in the clean sunshine were black.

'Where,' I asked abruptly, apropos of nothing, 'are the aboriginies?'

And not for the last time I heard that they were idle, drunken and stupid. And not for the last time I looked but I couldn't see one.

Chas drove us through tree-lined streets, past pretty gates and gardens, down to the water's edge where sometimes a yacht was moored. The mouth of the Swan River was as wide as a politician's, but the politician was smiling, and he'd gargled and cleaned his teeth.

No wonder Chas looked healthy, despite the hours he kept. Despite risking death by driving, despite the ingestion of beer. He was suntanned, still, in winter, and so was everybody, and the girls in the warehouse that housed all the books were advertisements for the seaside — their concession to the season was a thin veil of cardigans. Probably anyone who didn't look well or have all their teeth or a lacquered hairdo was removed from the streets by force, by night, and shut in a concentration camp. Keep West Australia tidy, and that includes West Australians.

The citizens weren't very beautiful (apart from Foghorn and Pansy) but they were a handsome people, and that looked good on the men.

The girls and the women radiated a frightening aura of well-groomed resilience — cyanide in their talcum powder, the iron fist in the white lace glove. When they were young they were overpowering, but after twenty-five they gradually became wirier and drier, and by the age of thirty they were putting things on doilies and starting to look remarkably like the San Andreas Fault. They wore what seemed to me a quite staggering amount of make-up, the sort of goo I wore in the 'sixties to achieve a fashionable pallor around my opossum eyes. As they grew older the make-up clogged in deep ravines and crevasses, and ladies of uncertain age shrivelled and hunched over their liquor like homunculi in jars.

Their ageing process was fascinating. What, between twenty and thirty, happened to their glorious, silky, glistening hair? What transformation turned it crisp and oilless and wiry, and left it in Caligula kiss-curls and brittle little knots? What turned their skins to parchment and their full lips to tight-drawn purses and created Father Time's footprints around their narrowed eyes?

The sun, of course, the sunshine. That same eternal sunshine that made them golden goddesses from the moment they were born. But surely it didn't account for the aridity of their brains?

'Yeah,' they kept saying. 'Beaut.'

The more I saw of the women, the more heatedly I warmed to their menfolk. Whatever they'd done as male chauvinist pigs they were only bringing the bacon home now.

Different and kinder things happened to them as they grew older — they had, after all, been singled out for the second coming, supporting above their waistbands bellies replete with the Heavenly Host.

Lines gave them the appearance of cosmic intelligence, as though their brows hadn't got furrowed trying to catch some barman's eye. Their skins were the colour of old leather. Their hair turned a thigh-melting grey. Their movements, never brisk except up and down the gullet, became languid to the point where they sat contentedly at green lights. Whatever senility might bring them, they would meet the onslaught relaxed.

'Relax' said the advertisements 'in the State of Excitement!' I gazed respectfully at the Perth skyline. If this was a state of excitement, what was the place like when it lay down? The idea was growing upon me that Australia, compared to England, might conceivably be less tense. The only things we did slower in England were growing older and getting out of debt.

Certainly we were quicker at jumping to conclusions, if the reactions of my bloke back home were anything to go by.

There had been a comfortable bundle of airmail letters waiting when I'd checked in at the Reception Desk, and having been allowed to telephone my Mother –

'Awwow! Alida? Is that you? Where are you?'

'I'm in Australia.'

'Awwow!'

'I'm 'phoning to say I've arrived and I'm all right.'

'Oooo, Alida! Awwow!' (My Mother, on the telephone, tends to be somewhat histrionic).

I'd telephoned my correspondent, and of course the bastard was out.

Contact having at last been made, I'd settled in to my stint of promotion. Days spent being nonplussed in radio stations: –

'What are all these T-Shirts for?'

'They give us a T-Shirt, we give 'em a mention. Wudduvyergot? Only these *books*?'

And taxi-cabs: –

'Hey, aintyer that mad woman they had on 6 PR this morning? Talkin' about *lavatories*?'

And book-shops: –

'Well, it makes a change to have something we can put in the window. Most of the stuff from your distributors is real *filth.*'

And in my hotel I was packing some time after

midnight, exhausted, and early next day to leave Perth. Stephen was talking to a chap from the local office, and I was trotting around them in a wrapper, looking at clothing, picking it up and putting it down. We were all fairly tired and moderately lubricated, and I'd been so kind to my throat I kept losing my case.

It had quickly been established that Stephen wasn't one of the buggers. He was ten years younger than me, quite humiliatingly capable, and regarded me as not just older than him but OLD. Despite the fact that I wasn't Australian, I was English. Usually I was slighted, but tonight I just felt he was right. It was very late and I was very tired, and the flight we were making next day would be no joke. Farther than London-New York and still over one country? I looked at my pillows, and Stephen looked at his watch.

'It'll be late afternoon in London now — I'll ring Henry.' And Stephen put in a call to his boss on my telephone. I went on ambling, and the local chap went on talking — a most interesting story about sheep-shearers, gum-boots and sheep.

The bedside 'phone burbled and Stephen hooked the receiver up. And there at the end of the line was my sceptical gentleman. Putting in a surprise call to say he loved me. And getting very steely at vast expense. I could hear his teeth gnashing as I took the 'phone over. His teeth were gnashing a hemisphere away.

'*What*' he demanded 'is a man doing in your bedroom? What's a man doing there *at your time of night*?'

'Darling! He's not a man, he's Stephen!' It says a lot for Stephen that he spoke to me after that.

The misunderstanding took a great deal of telephonic smoothing, and the removal of innocent youth to my dressing-room.

So I could defend myself and use four-letter words.

It was some time before Stephen could get through to London, and I didn't finish packing till gone three a.m.

I lay in bed, full of ire and Southern Comfort. (Stephen

had brought in a quart bottle, duty-free.) It had been such an innocent occasion. Even if I hadn't been too old, I'd have been too tired. What was I doing with a man in my room! 'Nothing!' I thought, flaking out. I was even too tired to attend to my own night-starvation. Things had come to a pretty dreadful, unlibidinous pass. How dare he! How *dare* he! I'd write a scathing missive – I'd have seven hours to do it, stuck up in wall-to-wall air. I could use filched hotel paper, and those purloined envelopes . . . I began to fall asleep, thoroughly warmed by my resentment. It was the first time since I'd landed that I'd fallen asleep feeling warm. The air-conditioning was so efficient that I went to bed in a jersey, and sat up in bed in the mornings eating breakfast in my coat.

A final thought shook me, drifting. Perhaps Pansy's big nipples were due to the air-conditioning.

CHAPTER TEN

The man between Perth and Sydney didn't mind when I slept on his shoulder.

'Go ahead' he said, looking surprised. Well, I suppose it did seem strange, in the middle of conversation, but he wasn't very scintillating, and I was very tired. And he had the most fabulous shoulder (I only found out about one).

After Sydney there was a change of luck and clavicle. I got a married couple, unfortunately they'd been to England, and despite donating them my TAA cake, I couldn't shut them up. Besides, I didn't have the man, I had the woman sitting next to me, and her shoulder was as inviting as dropping off on Mount Rushmore.

Stephen's physique wasn't a factor till the last leg of the journey, and by that time I was wide awake. I'd found Colleen McCullough stuck in the back of the seat in front. There she was on *Time* magazine, looking understandably creamy, and inside there was an article about how she'd written *Thorn Birds.* In nine weeks. And made a million. And she'd written it in nine weeks.

I wasn't sleeping on anybody. Nor yet was I communicating. I didn't trust myself to speak.

Somewhere between Adelaide and Brisbane, I was in a jealous torment. I had seen *Thorn Birds,* but I had not read it. I would have *liked* to read it, but I do most of my reading in bed and I dared not take this opus with me into the horizontal. What, and be crushed to death in the night by the ponderous weight of the volume?

I glared at the confident *Time* cover picture. I am the

slowest writer in the world, as anyone will know who waits for my cheques, and the idea of extruding that size of tome in nine years let alone nine weeks . . .

It was as well I'd written to my lover within an hour of take-off, and before I went to sleep on the obliging Australian. If I'd postponed my outburst of righteous indignation it would have admixed with professional fear and envy and set the paper alight.

I put away *Time* before I threw up and turned my hot thoughts to the journey. It had been a long one, and not getting Stephen had been a surprise. We'd arrived and checked in early at the airport, but no one would give us adjacent seats. When we asked, they tried to throw buckets of water over us. So the flights were spent, when I wasn't asleep, nodding and waving at one another, and meeting in transit lounges to compare our mutual thirst.

The first leg Australian had been quite OK though, and he'd had such a comfy shoulder. He apologised profusely when he had to get out at Sydney. One way and another, he'd been extraordinarily polite. Taking off his jacket so I could relax on his silk shirt . . .

Really, what with their doilies, and the coasters under their beer cans, I was beginning to think Australians were *all* extraordinarily polite. There was more than politeness: gentility. They'd cover piano legs.

Not that they covered their women. Glancing idly at Stephen, I saw what he was thumbing and wondered if his palms would grow hair.

Gate-fold ladies I usually envy, because they're so marvellously pretty, and because their breasts and buttocks seem immune to gravity. But the young ladies in Stephen's glossies were in serious danger. Their circumstances were a health hazard. They ran a grave risk of head colds, caught from the inside up.

'What the —' I spluttered, and then I remembered. Stephen wasn't being self-indulgent: he was relieving Mafeking, bringing the news from Ghent to Aix. Adult magazines for the sex-starved boys in Brisbane.

God, it must be a stiff city. Was it the sort of place where you couldn't hold hands in public? What would they do to me — a dedicated platonic clutcher?

I relinquished my ire and my sick-bag and started rummaging through my papers. *Somewhere* I must have that male prostitute's address.

CHAPTER ELEVEN

There were three men lounging, waiting for us in Brisbane. Not one of them looked sexually deprived. They looked comfortable, casual, relaxed, rather jolly and handsome.

Suffering from drought throat, an excess of seat-belts and claustrophobia, by comparison I was as calm as an electric fan.

They just hung there and let me gabble and gesticulate at them. You could see the thoughts forming behind their bland, sun-bronzed foreheads: 'Was she always like this or have they got rabies in Perth?'

And this was the city of hills, home from Rome, Vatican City? The clamped-down, strait-laced, sat-upon State of Queensland? I drew breath and sized up the at-eased Reception Committee. If they were constrained they'd certainly been taking the tablets: they were as tense as fifteen-year-old elastic bands.

'We-ell,' they grinned, and there were introductions. Michael Ryan, the boss, and thin Ron and tubby Warry. And my luggage was hefted, and did I think I could manage my own handbag? I was told to relax, calm down, we could look around Brisbane, and abruptly I realised how tiredness had made me jumpy. Tiredness, and the continual repetitive story re-telling, and always having to be so English but *nice*. And Chas forever 'phoning up from the foyer. And watching Chas permanently breaking his permanent diet. And being convinced I was the sole reason for his comfort eating — I was nervous enough, but Chas was more nervous than me.

Maybe this lot had nerves too, but they seemed to have left them at home.

I walked out into the clear night and through real air into the car park. Real air, after air-conditioning. I stood for a moment, just breathing, ignoring the door, but Ron clucked a little and then there I was in a seat-belt. The click of the clasp brought an instant, Pavlovian response: I gripped the edge of the seat and clenched my teeth. After all, this was Australia, wasn't it? The land of the Kamikaze with rear-wheel drive?

But Ron was leaving the parking space without using a vocal, and without any rib-smashing semaphore involving elbows. His attitude to the other traffic was live and let live. The other traffic wasn't going anywhere.

From time to time a mild frown or a blink bore witness to deep inner turmoil, and he'd murmur softly 'We-ell, suppose Mick knows where we're off to now.'

Mick and Warry and Steve were in the car that didn't have my luggage, and we were chasing each other gently into Brisbane. Race-courses, race-courses . . . but we were aiming inevitably towards the river. To floodlit bridges like fluorescent strands of pulled toffee. To bands and sweeps and stretches, and moonbursts of bounced light.

Ron explained, as we drove, how the river meandered, and as we drove I imagined Indian ink ox-bows, and mapping pen meanders drawn twenty years ago. But that was for homework about the Mississippi. And this was another continent — this inky river was real. Here were meanders like fingers, clutching and clasping, and the city had put on its gloves and shaken soft hands. It had arranged itself as it liked between the thumbs and the fingers, and what it liked was so pleasant that the river didn't seem to mind.

'Water!' I marvelled to Ron. 'I've never seen so much water!'

'Not even in England? I thoughtyer got wet all the time.'

But most English water comes out of the sky. Brisbane's leapt out of the ground. What didn't flow under bridges was pumping and prinking through fountains, in great surges of green, blue and pink. It flourished and skirled, it did bumps and grinds, its foam naiads were drum majorettes. Hopping about and shaking, pulsating rah-rah-rah-splat. It was the most riveting — the *only* local vision of get up and go energy. Probably people hadn't always been that languid — they'd come over tired watching the water rushing about. Every corner you smoothed round, every downhill you coasted — there it was: raining in pink. Wherever you looked, a multi-coloured volcano. An eruption of inexhaustible rising damp.

The impact didn't just slow you down, it struck you mute.

You, not me — I've had a cut throat and not been deprived of speech. But even my jabber was quietened. And Ron's method of driving relaxed me: accelerating in Brisbane proved to be taking your foot off the brake. So I sat, with an occasional squeal of appreciation. All I had to do was sit and stare. When we weren't gliding up Expressways, we were discovering golden-lit buildings and circling squares. When we weren't gazing at lights across sparkling water, we were gazing at water across the sparkling lights.

It was like being at a World's Fair without too many people: a great big, beautiful store that had shut out the crowds. There was traffic, of course — constant, ruminative traffic. I noticed the fountains rather out-numbered the cars.

'The Queen opened that one.' Ron, almost galvanised, pointing. 'Kinyersee?'

'You mean the one that isn't working?'

Tactfully, we left the matter aside.

The hotel foyer was tucked deeply back in the throat of an arcade; we'd only be there a short time, so I wouldn't have mail. But irrationally I'd hoped, and felt cheated by a key and no letters. In Perth fat envelopes had been there each day, from home. Although I knew we'd arranged to skip this *poste restante,* the fact that he *had* was enough to rekindle my ire. Jealous and nagging and not even writing a line! The illogic of this was supremely satisfying, and I handed a clerk my scathing airmail to post.

It did flit through my head, about an hour later, that it might have been worse tonight if he'd made a call. We were lying on the beds eating oysters and lobster, and the blokes had sent out for cold beer, and brandy for me.

'Aw, cripes, yer won't even get up to the Gold Coast! Comin' all this way and not seein' the Gold Coast —' Warry looked like a bear. He shook his head: an incredulous Teddy. 'It's a bloody crime.'

'The Gold Coast? They're still bathing?'

'There's always bathing!' Mick appealed to an oyster: 'Listen, it's got to be the most beautiful beach yer've ever seen.'

'It started raining in Perth,' I grumbled, round some lettuce. 'They said I'd brought English weather.'

'Yer couldn't if yer tried — not to Queensland.'

I brooded on the bleak return I'd made to polo-neck sweaters. 'The weather's good now?'

'The weather's beaut now!'

I flinched. 'I can wear dresses?'

Mick rang his wife for confirmation, putting his finger in the dial very carefully. And yes, it was relayed, I could wear dresses. His wife sounded understanding, for one a.m.

Everyone seemed so sweet, and so free and easy. Fuddy-duddy indeed! I kissed them all goodnight. Strait-laced Brisbane — I thought they were all lovely. And they told funny stories . . . Which is — indirectly — how I came to say bullshit.

The morning sun was glorious over the roof-tops. I put on a summer dress, left off my stockings, and *froze*.

'Wha-wha-wha-what'sh-happened?Wh-wh-wh-where's the w-warm w-weather?' My teeth were chattering by the time I'd reached the car.

'Can't understand it. The temperature dropped off suddenly in the night.' Mick's handsome face ruffled – momentarily – and then smoothed. 'Id'll warm up later. Look, it's a beaudaful day.' The day was certainly beautiful, although chilly, and Brisbane was squaring up under third degree light. It was the sort of light that finds out a lady's age. The moon had gone and with it the romance of darkness: Brisbane was taking hormones for the menopause.

Her mellow buildings had spread when wide hips were the fashion. Now their lower storeys were squeezed into boutiques. Sets and salons of stately Victorian dowagers, lifting their skirts over patent leather, rhinestone-studded drawers.

Oh, but here was the river, and even piercing daylight couldn't spoil that. Curving, vanishing, reappearing water, passing back-stroke under bridge after bridge after bridge. Suspension bridges, bridges that ran on from freeways, spans and arches and shapes that were stolid or light.

We were heading towards the Australian Broadcasting Commission, coasting the rim of Coronation Drive, and Mick pointed out the riverbanks – reclaimed from a sprawling mess of industrial waste and wharves. They were to be landscaped, he said – they looked like landscape already. I come from London. To me, it's landscape when it's green.

'You can picnic,' said Mick. 'Hey, and you should look at that.' He slowed and parked. 'The old Regatta. Bit sorry for itself now, but that was a great old pub.' It stood on a corner, behind interlaced verandahs. A balconied building of a type I would see everywhere. I didn't know that then, gaping at white metal crochet. I'd never seen wrought-iron work so overwrought.

But I was to see it. I was to see it in dreams, and waking, constantly, with my eyes shut. Like the word 'beaut' its usage came to affect me strangely. I was told in every city how it originated. Even now I cringe from cards of New Orleans – it was architectural aversion therapy.

When ships sailed to Australia, they took along cast-iron as ballast, and wrought-iron work decorates a lot of old houses and pubs. The first time you see it, you think it's quaint – olde worlde and enchanting. It can be pretty in the right surroundings, and held in check. The Regatta Hotel was a formidable presentation, gracious and spacious in a perfect situation, and I felt like applauding: all it lacked were the crinolines on the porch.

It wasn't till I'd been force-fed five hundred more examples that I dyspeptically realised what the style looked like; it looked as though a demented, half-trained pastry chef had run amuck over a house with a loaded icing pipe.

'We'll leave the car here,' said Mick. 'Little way – we'll just walk to the studios.'

In two minutes the walk had become a canter, my teeth were jingling, my lenses were rimed and I was tripping on my goose-flesh.

'Can't understand it!' panted Mick, rounding a driveway. 'Sunny like this and how it's got so cold –'

'I t-t-t-*told* y-you.' We collapsed, shuddering, inside the glass doors. 'I've got a sore throat, Stephen's got rheumatism – I'm an English jinx, it was *pouring* when I left Perth.'

'We-ell, you won't be a jinx here.' Mick smiled and tapped at a door with his frozen knuckles. 'You'll see – they're a real good crowd, nice people. We've always had a good relationship.'

A bright girl appeared. Her clipboard was dazzling.

Mick said 'Hello' and 'Michael Ryan', and introduced Stephen, and said 'This is Alida Baxter, for the Gary Orde Show.'

Mick and Stephen were given chairs at the back of the studio, and I was seated opposite the important Mr Orde. He turned out to be a young brother of Father Christmas, rounded, presentable and inclined to say 'Ho-ho-ho.' The interview went happily, I thought, thanks to the interviewer, who was not only full of good cheer, but intelligent and kind. This seemed to be the rule with ABC — the national network. It was the commercial shows that had you on as steak tartare.

I enjoyed myself, the whole thing went so well. True, at one point a stillness seemed to settle. A cold stillness like a cloud of ectoplasm, that obscured for a moment Mr Orde's Father Christmas face. It went as it came, but then I could feel it rearing behind me: deep-frozen stillness, hunching behind my neck.

I glanced round swiftly and saw Mick sitting rigid, grey as a sheet. Stephen was bored and eyeing the talent in the control room. He hadn't noticed but Mick must have had some sort of stroke. No . . . Thank goodness, he was moving, the colour returning —

'And how long will you be in Brisbane?'

I turned back to Gary Orde.

The interview ended, mine host tired and older, Father Christmas on Boxing Day. But he'd given us a plug for a book-signing session; we thanked him. We thanked the assistant; her nails were white on her blinding clipboard. We got outside, but Mick still hadn't recovered. He was distracted all the way to the car. If he'd had more hair he'd have looked like my ex-husband, the time he learned I'd bought him a new shirt but no more gin.

When we were in our seat-belts, Michael broke it to me gently. 'You'll be signing books at Myers.' His voice was going — he gripped the wheel. 'Myers is a good store, Myers is old-fashioned, the assistants wear black dresses —'

'The men or the women?'

'Myers has ladies, not women! It's a respectable store.' He floundered, and went up an octave. 'FOR GOD'S SAKE DON'T BLASPHEME.'

'No, Mick.' It must be brain-damage. Obviously. Humour him, up to a point.

He started the car. That gave him trouble. Finding the ignition with that little key. 'Has anyone told you about the way we are in Queensland?'

'Well – '

'Maybe we're not so permissive.'

'I wouldn't say – '

'We've got our own way of doing things.'

'You've got a male prostitute!'

The car had started but now it stalled. 'Alida, don't use bad language. Especially when you're interviewed – don't swear, please don't!'

'I didn't swear! Did I swear? Stephen?'

'Swearing, what swearing? Christ, these fucking shows, don't they get on your tits.'

Mick appeared to be in some difficulty with his motor. 'Alida, you said bullshit to Gary Orde.'

'But everybody says bullshit – it's the only Australian comment. I heard it on the 'plane, I heard nothing else on the boat – don't you talk to me about bad language. On the boat I brought somebody the wrong drink and I apologised and he said "Christ, we wring out shitty rags".'

'Alida – '

'You tell an Australian he can't swear and you might as well sew up his mouth.'

'Australia's different from Queensland!'

'Michael – '

'We don't do much swearin' in Queensland.'

'Michael, my God – '

'Or blasphemin'. You can't blaspheme on Queensland Radio!'

'I didn't blaspheme, I said bullshit. He wanted to know whether writing was easy and I said anyone who says

BASTARD IN
BULLSHIT OUT
SOUND MIXER

writing is easy is talking a load of —'

'I know, but you don't have to say it!'

'I don't have to say it back home. I've picked up a native expression. It's like Vegemite and Pie Floaters — it's the Australian curse.'

Stephen leaned over the back seat. 'And bastard. You could call someone a bastard — that wouldn't get up his nose.'

'We-ell —' Michael was steering. If we hadn't been in the car with him, he might easily have driven away.

'That's right. Bastard's a term of affection.' I appealed to him. 'Isn't it? Isn't it a term of affection?'

'We still wouldn't say it in front of women. We don't swear much in front of women. Alida, *this is Queensland.*'

'Oh.' I collapsed, castrated. Everyone swore in front of me.

'But even in Queensland you can call someone a bastard.' Stephen was still there, stuck in a groove. 'He wouldn't bash you.'

Michael was silent.

'Would he bash you if you called him a —'

Wild screech of hot rubber.

There are miracles in Queensland. Michael swore, *and* he missed the truck.

CHAPTER TWELVE

The book-signing became livelier with the mad woman, the TV news-men, the arc-lights and the invasion by a jolly Melbourne Football Team. The mad woman was charming — she bought me some dahlias. And one young couple came specially, because I'd said *that word*.

Michael, fully recovered except for head-shaking, had made appointments with Stephen and handed me over to Ron. And Ron, relieved several hours later, had handed me over to a guide-book and lounged purposefully back towards work.

It was mid-afternoon: only traces now of the warm weather that Ron had assured me was going on outside the stores. As soon as I had gone in, out had come the sunshine. You couldn't have me and the sun simultaneously.

Wary, I'd taken the time to collect a scarf and a jacket, and wasn't too cold now as I walked the arcaded streets.

In how many sunny countries have I wandered in arcades, and wondered why the English don't have them to ward off the rain. It's the same with roofed-in porches and verandahs. Apart from a few full-frontals at the seaside, we British only see them south of Dieppe.

I stood musing over my map by the Anzac memorial, as the shadows deepened in the gulf of the lower square. Smells of metal and dust from the Central Station behind me, not late enough yet for the brilliant lights to be on.

The soft dusk suited this part of the city: dusk is always a good time to think about wars. 'The memorial — a circular colonnade of Doric columns.' Melting beige now, tonight it would spring up, well lit. If you walked down the steps beneath it, into the square, you came to a statue of a sad, martial man on a horse, and that was the memorial to the South African War. A breeze on my face. Why am I such a push-over for men in puttees? Scrolls of honour in churches, First World War tunes from a bandstand, snatches of quick-step marching on indistinct film . . .

I tightened the scarf and walked faster. Ron and Michael had both explained the streets — the ladies' names in the city, regal and loyal, tilting gently down to the river's South Reach. The gentlemen's names — Edward, Albert, George, William — a royal flush — pacing briskly across the paths of the ladies. Heading towards the bosky Botanic Gardens. Not surprisingly, in view of its secretive shrubs. Mick had shown Stephen and me around them, and we'd nearly lost Stephen to a stroller, who'd asked to see his telephoto lens.

The New Zealand Tourist Office — I passed it, planning. I'd be going to New Zealand on my way home. Queen Street — towards the foot of it stood my hotel. No point in going back yet, when there'd be no letters. I trotted as far as the lamp-posts and walked round Queens Park.

The hotel in Sydney before I saw another new letter. And England was such a terribly long way away. My Mother couldn't hear properly when I tried to 'phone her, and addresses and welfare were relayed in wire-splitting screams. Better or worse than depth-charged calls from old Jump to Conclusions? I vacillated between missing him and getting miffed. And at that moment I was getting decidedly chilly; get back, have some tea, shake off this dying-sun mood.

When I opened the door of my room, on the floor lay a cable. Six words — and I wanted a dance and a drink. Have a shower, put my feet up, watch TV — we were going out this evening. Amazing how much could be changed by those faint, squared-up words.

'The shoes,' breathed Stephen, formless in the darkness. 'Did you see the *shoes*?'

It was my first experience of an Australian dinner/cabaret. My impression was, it would have been good somewhere else. Where it could have responded to the right treatment. Tonight's audience should have been up for hire as a unit, a Hydra to scare to death your wealthy aunt. Inert, they were demolishing the comedian. He must have sweated off at least ten pounds.

Averting my eyes from the carnage, I groped round my steak. Would I ever, I wondered, come to terms with Australian menus? With hors d'oeuvres called entrées and incredible portions of meat?

Not that I'd been the first to boggle in this way. A century before, Trollope had commented on the eating habits of the immigrant to Queensland.

'The Irishman, who has come from the unchanging perpetuity of potatoes to a plethora of meat, teaches himself to believe within twelve months that he never sat down to dinner at home without a beefsteak or a roast fowl. I came to a little dispute once with a working man at Rockhampton. "If you knew what it was," he said, "to have eaten mutton three times a day, day after day, week after week, month after month, you would not come here and tell us that we ought to be contented with our condition."'

Was the comedian contented with his condition? He'd obviously migrated here. There was a merciful outbreak of singing, and then the curtains were pulled across, bulging, and there was a short interval.

'You're *sure*,' I began, reopening a conversation that the cabaret had interrupted.

'It's a break for us!' Mick's wife protested gamely. 'I just hope you won't be tired out by the girls.'

'A family weekend – at the Gold Coast? Building sand

castles with kids?' Stephen had picked up his jacket. 'You know what you're doing' – which he did not believe. 'When I get to Sydney I'm driving up to the Blue Mountains.' He'd straightened his tie at the mirror and looked at me pityingly.

It was the thought of the flight to Sydney, really, more than anything. After only thirty-six hours, yet another 'plane? Another sore throat, closing up in the air-conditioning. It was getting clearer daily I'd travelled too soon after losing my tonsils. And in Sydney it wouldn't be chilly, it'd be bloody cold. If the weather was cool in Queensland, there'd be ice forming in New South Wales.

So when Mick had first made the mention, I'd thrown myself at the chance: driving with his family to spend Saturday down at the Gold Coast – a break, walking on beaches, away from the city, an early night. I didn't have to be in Sydney until Sunday afternoon. I could fly straight from Coolangatta – get myself settled in fresh for the work that would start on Monday.

Only now I allowed myself a brief tickle of worry.

'Thank Heaven . . .' sang the comedian, in a straw hat and accent.

The audience glared sullenly through the foot-lights. Two couples fought, and someone having a birthday wept in the cheesecake.

'Thank Heaven . . .'

Probably I'd be massacred, from what I'd seen of little girls.

CHAPTER THIRTEEN

'Just because *she* isn't tall she reckons being tall doesn't amount to very much.' Lisa, having dismissed her best friend, drowned her sorrows in pink lemonade. In case I'd forgotten my lenses, she said 'Have you seen all the desserts?' Blonde, with a perfect face and a permanent hairbrush, Lisa was the quieter, more introspective, of the two sisters. Of course it was fairly easy: her sister had built-in stereo.

She frowned over a spoonful. 'Mummy, do I like caramel custard?' The forehead crumpled under the silk fringe, the eyes were darkened by the long lashes. In a few years' time that same frown would be turning strong men inside out.

Peta-Marie had been quiet for two minutes. This must have meant that she was eating. When Peta-Marie was talking, she didn't pause to breathe. She was the only person I'd ever met who could talk that long without turning blue. I believe it's a technique of singers, but Peta-Marie had it perfected. She could have taught Frank Sinatra, and I was learning a thing or two.

'We're all loyal and we show our loyalty and support him don't you think you should show your loyalty Alida and Lisa's loyal too and he's got such beautiful eyes and he's so nice and he smiled right at me isn't he beautiful Lisa?'

Lisa said flatly 'I *don't* like caramel custard.'

'Well, you don't have to eat it then, darling.'

'He's wonderful and when we went to see him there

were people just suffocating and we got separated and there were thousands of people and we might not have got out *alive* Alida are you sure you haven't heard of him?'

Lisa studied a nail-bed. 'May I go and wash my hands?'

'Not for a moment, darling, I'm just finishing my coffee.'

'I can go on my own, I know where it is.'

'He's terribly popular and he has the most beautiful hair don't you think that hair is important and intelligence but his eyes just —'

'I'd like you to wait for me, darling.'

'Why can't I go on my own? I could go on my own, Mummy.'

'Oh he's just so beautiful he's a really beautiful person I wish we lived in Sydney because Queensland's so backward really it doesn't have hardly any discothèques —'

'Please sit down and wait for me, darling.'

'I wouldn't take long, honest.'

'As soon as I'm grown up I'm going to Sydney I wish we lived there already it's just so beautiful and so forward thinking and Queensland doesn't have any educational opportunities —'

'You always take so long, darling.'

'I wouldn't, I promise.'

'When we were in Sydney we stayed in this hotel and whenever we were hungry we could ring down for sandwiches we had five different kinds each and chocolate milk shakes I think Sydney's the most beautiful place I've ever seen Queensland's so backward it's just so old-fashioned I wish we lived in New South Wales —'

'You may not go alone, Lisa.'

'Peta-Marie can come with me.'

'Peta-Marie won't stop you using that hot-air hand-drier sixteen times!'

Dark-haired Mick, his fair-haired wife, dark, nervy Peta-

Marie, fair, slender Lisa. We had left Brisbane when it was raining ('Raining now. Whatcher done to the weather around here?') and arrived in sunshine at the Gold Coast. Not a long drive, made even shorter by lack of boredom in the back seat. The two girls were slender as reeds and obviously starving. They ate daintily, but continually, from the moment Mick started the car. After the first dozen packets of crispy golden munchies I concluded they were the type that starved themselves at meal-times — a conclusion that was shattered long before they got round to desserts. Lisa didn't like caramel custard, but the exception was notable.

'How on earth —' I asked their mother.

'They're just always hungry — it's like feeding a plague of locusts. Not more chocolate, girls, *please*. You know it makes you break out.'

The girls politely offered me shares of everything they opened. If I'd indulged myself in ten per cent I'd have put on half a stone. Perhaps they took after their mother, who was enviably slim without dieting. Or perhaps they burned it up, growing. Or in leading an active life. When Lisa was sitting she thought a great deal and when Peta was sitting she bounced.

'Oh look there's the castle is that like an English castle?'

I peered out of the window at a winsome Walt Disney spire. Snow-White-style turrets, was that a drawbridge? And a *chair-lift*? 'No, not really, ours are all broken down.'

'*Really*?' Peta-Marie tried vainly to hide her shock and horror. 'Did that happen in the war?'

'No, it happened before that. Most of our castles are old.'

'And they haven't been looked after?' Horror had spread round the car.

'Well, yes, but they've had a long time to fall down. And they must have been knocked about when they were fought over — nothing's changed, we've always fought amongst ourselves. And people are careless with

historical buildings. They don't think about history, they strike a match and there you are.' The sun shone on the glossy ribbon development. 'We've always taken old buildings for granted, I suppose.'

There was a two-minute silence while everyone strove for a topic, desperate for some bland subject to solace the guilty. It was Lisa who eventually opened a packet. 'When you get off the chair-lift,' she asked me, 'do they have ghosts?'

The castle protected hotels and holiday apartments, laid back in the warmth on the edge of the vast, sandy beach. Waves ribbed the pale waste, a desert now in the off-season, and few visitors strolled round the palm trees or cut-price fruit stores. Our hotel was full of the elderly, come from chillier climates to ease their joints in this kind air and spend the winter in the sun.

A quiet winter. The ribbon was fairly narrow and the country took over behind it. Off in the not-too-far distance rose slowly rolling hills. Up on one of those hill-sides I'd been introduced to a koala. Well, how could I come to Australia without meeting one of those?

At Burleigh Heads there was an animal sanctuary — emus, kangaroos, koala bears, a wombat. Even that extraordinary thing, a duck-billed platypus.

We had driven up into the dense trees and left the car on the terraced hillside. The woman who gave out the tickets apologised for the platypus.

'But that's a shame.' Mick was crestfallen. 'This lady's come all the way from England. She won't be out here again —'

'Yeah, I'm sorry but the platypus is crook.'

But I did get to see a koala, and to take a drowsy photograph. It pawed its sleepy eyes, dozy and dribbling over its keeper's shoulder as he fed it vitamins in a mess of sticky syrup. I touched the thick fur, soft as powder-puffs should be, and sniffed the warm, slightly nauseous smell of the sweetness in the tin cup. In clearings, kangaroos scratched and loped, and lazily agreed to be petted, and grubby emus stepped about with their beaks just above the ground. From terrace to terrace the gum trees and swarming shrubs led down to a valley, and between scarlet flowers I saw the coast. Blue and gold and deep, green-ink greenness. Queensland didn't need botanical gardens; the whole State was an open-air hothouse running amuck. Sultry and humid for most of the year, never truly wintry — there was a positive threat of take-over by vegetation. I had the feeling that if I dropped a match, it'd sprout. And whatever it sprouted would be in the best Kodachrome.

Small wonder coloured light played through the water in Brisbane — your eyes became so addicted, they had to be constantly feasted on rich colour. And in Queensland nature had hooked, and then pandered to eyes. Paint-pots had emptied in gallons on trees, birds and bushes. The sunset was a flamingo's funeral pyre. Out for an evening walk, I rounded a headland, and the flames on the water took my breath away.

As the 'plane lifted away that Sunday from Coolangatta, I looked down on car tops that quickly gave way to verdure. To a rippling mass of inward-turned, tropical forest. And I remembered the bars of light, corrugated by surf.

I remembered the Ryans taking me to the bird sanctuary at Currumbin, where the peacocks weren't half as bright as the native Lorikeets.

I remembered the crash of the waves beneath my hotel window, and the lone pair of dapper, bespectacled Japanese tourists, photographing each other on the bare beach at dawn.

I remembered the girls bringing me sea-shells and bottle-brushes. And I wanted very much not to see a city.

CHAPTER FOURTEEN

Particularly one in which I'd arrive all alone.

Apart from the rest of the passengers. And the crowds on the concourse. If there were crowds on the concourse, and not just a few loiterers. Airports are, in this, exactly like railway stations: whenever you travel, they're either too large or too small.

I didn't look forward, alone, to the inevitable gritty procedures — the wait, the invisible trolleys, the next wait, the marathon walks. The blood-sport reclaiming mugged luggage. Waiting poised by a chute or a ramp or a belt or a merry-go-round. Watching the trek of an orphaned hold-all. Every baggage-hall of my life, it's got there before me — that hold-all. Unclaimed, a flying dutchman. Check, with off-white handles and a central sag.

The central sag lurked in my disposition. I didn't even know what Sydney Airport looked like. Glass, vinyl tiles, migraine illumination? Concrete? The usual changing room — London for Frankfurt, Bombay for Athens. Echoes and untraceable draughts that never refreshed the tired air.

I didn't know how complex it was, or how far outside the city, and nobody could possibly meet me — they wouldn't know which flight I'd be on. Stephen was in the Blue Mountains, I'd only had brief telephone talks with the Sydney people . . .

Unlike Lisa, I didn't want to go anywhere on my own.

We wouldn't be at the hotel we'd planned — some

bookings mix-up. So where and when could I collect my overseas mail? I sank lower into my firm, resistant seat. All these matters had been in my head when I left Brisbane, but the break with the Ryan family had deferred my mind.

'Tea?' smiled the air hostess (flash-bulb teeth). 'Coffee?' Tea from a tray, in a cup that was more aesthetic, because there'd been some spare seats in First Class. I sipped, and sighed. Obviously an egalitarian beverage, miraculously infused to leave you drier than before.

'Wuddya like a biscuit?' The hostess was on elastic. Every time you lost her, you got her back again. She beamed past me, radiant. She looked as though she'd just been pinched by somebody with money. I peered sourly down the 'plane. It must have been one of the crew.

I'd been in hospital with an air hostess, losing my tonsils, and when she wasn't throwing up she was feverishly quoting their rules. The rules sounded pretty queer, mumbled in delirium, but they didn't sound any better when her temperature went down. One kept me awake at nights, long after she was snoring. They're not allowed to say 'Peanuts?' because that sounds suggestive, so when they serve you drinks and nuts they have to say 'Savouries?'.

I used to spend my detonsilled nights, in pain and sleepless, trying to work out what there was about 'Peanuts?' to misconstrue.

Of course I remembered the famous case of my friend and the explanation — when he led his little daughter step by step through the facts of life. He thought he'd do it all properly — whatever it was, use the name for it. After an hour he had her completely convinced men have got something called a 'Peanuts'.

She misheard him — supposing passengers misheard the stewardesses? Being airborne can do strange things to your ears. Not to mention what the thrum does to your libido. Perhaps that was why they played safe and

avoided 'Peanuts?'. They didn't want lady passengers at the crew's flies.

And there were the men — what would male passengers think was on offer? Might 'Peanuts?' raise hope in the stunted of a Jumbo transplant? A new British Airways service? A club that was *really* mile high?

'Madam?' A uniformed figure was bobbing beside me. 'Madam?' It was lady elastic. 'Wuddya like some more tea?'

'What? Oh! Oh, no,' I said. 'Thank you.' Surely to God we must be there by now.

'Good afternoon' crackled instantly through the cabin. 'This is your — — speaking — — fine day in Syd — — visibility — — temperature — — ney harbour on the — — — — side.'

We bent to look, obediently. And landed. And dreared into the building. No letters, no one to meet me.

'Hello,' said Stephen, behind me. 'Have a good time?'

Driven back by snow, he'd given up the idea of the mountains and had come to the airport on the chance that I'd be on this flight. I'd never been so grateful to trot after my cases, but '*Snow*?' I squeaked at his shoulders in disbelief. My face was still brown and rosy from Coolangatta. I squinted through the glass doors. 'What's it doing out there?'

'It's all right *here*. Christ, it's warm. The sun's shining.'

I crossed my fingers. Probably hail by nightfall. I'd been lucky up on the Gold Coast, but that was the first time, and I'd been quick out from under, before my presence took effect. Did the country always react by deep-freezing invaders? If Australia had played England at weather, they'd have won every time.

We walked to where he'd left the hired car parked, and Stephen was right, it was very warm here. Following the highway into Sydney, the sun came like a brick at the windscreen.

'You should have come to the Gold Coast, we didn't

build castles. I met a koala bear, and the *food,* Stephen —'

'Christ!'

'Stephen?'

'I can see it but I can't get at it!' He drummed his fingers, frustrated and furious.

Just in case, I covered everything. Then I said 'Eh?'

'The hotel.' He ground the gears testily. 'The bloody hotel.'

We were driving amongst the grey stacks of the city high-rises. This close, the lay-out was almost as bad as London. Every time you got near to a street you were heading away from it, and what fascinated me was the lack of four sides to a block. Lots of blocks had only three sides, but there were others with fives sides, or seven. By the time one block had produced nine turn-left signs and seventeen corners, we were both slightly querulous and more than a little restive. I was making feeble, croaking 'tea' noises and Stephen, understandably, wanted something to eat. No one had said 'Wuddya like a biscuit?' to him in hours; God knows what would have happened if anyone had proffered him 'Peanuts?'. On the other hand, and ignoring his stomach, he wouldn't give up.

'I can see it,' he yelped at me. 'Can't you see it?'

'Yes,' I said. I could, lying flat on my back with my head through the window. At least, lying in that position, I could see the top. A tall hotel. And if I'd realised it was a high-priced concentration camp, I'd have checked in to steal a blanket and then slept in Hyde Park.

'Got it!' Stephen zoomed up a ramp and did a pit-stop by a sleek entrance. That was when I made the mistake: not realising, I climbed out of the car.

We were only going to wash — freshen up and dump our cases — we needed refuelling and a sight of Sydney, and I wanted tea. But induction took longer than we'd imagined, what with the pledges to be signed at Reception, although they were magnanimous and didn't test our blood. An aggrieved porter led us to a lift and got out at the twenty-fourth storey; from his attitude it was apparent they put the dross on these lower floors.

No sooner had he gone than I realised that my room was like a sauna; I tried twiddling with the fancy thermostat, but that didn't do a bit of good. Have a wash — that might make me cooler.

'Excuse me,' I said, towel in one hand (I was using it to wipe away the sweat). 'But the air-conditioning isn't working in my room.'

The receiver made an exasperated humpf.

'I'd open the window but it's stuck —'

'Please don't open the window! Don't *touch* the window, Madam. Security.'

'All right, I won't touch it —' The towel caught the sweat that was running off my shoulder. 'How about someone else? Can someone else touch it? Can you please send someone up here to touch it for me?'

'Madam, it's not hotel policy to open the windows.'

'Then why has mine got a handle and a hinge?'

'The handle and the hinge are obsolete, Madam. We have a controlled temperature and air-conditioning —'

'No you don't!' I mopped the beads off the receiver. 'You don't even have *air* — not in my room.'

The receiver sighed boredly. 'We'll send up an engineer, Madam.'

'Would you, please. It's like Dante's Inferno in here.'

At least we were going out — I wiped myself over — and with luck it'd be fixed; they'd have all afternoon.

We found the harbour when Stephen took off the hand-brake, but after we'd found it we had to find somewhere to park. Then I found a map and opened it to see where we were going, and found a shot of a jigsaw, seen through a wide-angle lens.

'Something the matter?'

'No, just whimpering.' I'd found another map, opened it and closed it again — another shot: different jigsaw, same lens.

Better to forget maps and follow trustingly behind

Stephen, who was confident and said this way to the Opera House. I thought his aim was marvellous, till I heard what he was hearing; Stephen was following the sound of a military band. Down a slope, round a bend, along a covered walkway — sun on white concrete, the air taking marches and jigs. Crowds were milling past us in the sunshine, some people quick to the music, others slowed by the walk from their cars. Above the promenade, across from the Harbour Bridge, the Opera House spread its white arcs to warm in the sun. Tourists swarmed round it, their dark shapes obscuring its front steps, or were still on the piazza, heads inclined, listening to the band.

Stephen went to fetch tea and I found a table — a white nursery shape on the promenade, beneath the Opera House, outside the brisk café. Seagulls flapped for titbits, kids yelled for ice-cream and were held up for a better view. Steamers cut back and forth to the bays and yachts with bright spinnakers hovered and rushed on the dark, glassy water.

Being on a diet, Stephen confined himself to chocolate éclairs. 'There's something you've got to see,' he said. 'Speakers Corner.'

I poured myself another cup. 'You mean like in Hyde Park?'

'They've got a Hyde Park here and a Speakers Corner. I'll take you over, I think it's in the Domain.'

'Afterwards can we see the hotel we'd have stayed at?'

He looked at me, smeared with chocolate. 'What for?'

'So I can pick up my post.'

The Domain was a sloping greensward, rising from the Expressway towards the bulk of the Art Gallery. Lakes of hecklers were grouped round two principal speakers, and the one that attracted me most had an untainted English accent.

'Lazy bloody Aussies!' he was screaming at a policeman. 'They open their mouths to say G'day and that's exhausted their vocabulary!'

The crowd laughed, united. From the murmurs drifting about me, I'd already picked six languages and not one was Australian English.

'They think they're copying the British, walking their little dogs. Little dogs!' He foamed at the mouth. 'Shit-boxes on legs! And walking 'em isn't British. The British keep their dogs indoors, where they can get at 'em, to kick 'em. That's how they hit back at the world. Only good thing they ever did was to fight the bloody Germans!' There followed the speaker's war record, and a tirade directed against Hitler.

An excited little man kept jumping about in the front row, and at every anti-Hun comment he emitted a shriek of 'Yes! Yes!' This, surprisingly, failed to please the speaker, who treated all interruptions alike, as though they were crass heckling. 'Gawdstrewth,' he fumed. 'Can't you shut up? Are you foreign or something? What are you?'

The little man gazed adoringly and straightened his suit. 'I'm Polish!'

'Only good thing the Germans did was trying to wipe out the Poles!'

People held back the little man and somebody sat on his head. Meanwhile the orator dwelt with hate on Spics and Wops and Eyeties, Niggers and Wogs, the Yellow Peril, mad Micks, mean Jocks, drunk Taffs, and Yanks.

More and more people were holding each other down. Fathers of families were being restrained by their women. The policemen moved closer, slowly, and looked totally unmenacing.

A Japanese tourist took a quick snap and was challenged to explain Pearl Harbour. A group of Spaniards were told that Latin lovers are impotent. Every time the little man crawled to his feet it was to hear 'Dirty Pole!' thundered at him, whereupon some well-wisher would sit on his head again.

Just when I thought the speaker would be deposed by a

...AND AS FOR BLOODY POLICEMEN...
I HATE EVERYTHING

lynch-mob, the policemen took a thumb each from their belts and shooed the whole crowd away.

'Well,' I said to Stephen. 'That was interesting. Can we —'

'Get your letters now.'

Stephen drove me to Double Bay, which was home from home down to the beigels, and collected my fat stack of letters and took me to have yet more tea.

Beyond the window, expensive boutiques and delicatessens. Hairdressers, restaurants and furniture shops.

Inside, smart little women with rings and middle-aged men with cigar ash sat on banquettes under soft lights and dipped silver forks in pastries.

A young matron to our left shrieked at her girl friend: 'Didn't I tell you it doesn't like me, that chopped herring?' and then fell to discussing her stocks and shares.

An English comedian rattled his Sunday paper and a waitress passed by with a tray of strudel and cheesecake.

'Oh, Stephen,' I said. 'Isn't it lovely? Golders Green.'

'That's why Henry wanted you to stay here.'

'And now we're stuck in that concrete monolith.'

But more liquid brightened me up and reduced my neck glands, and made me amenable to being driven to see more bays. Each distinctive, hilly, gemlike and enchanting. I surreptitiously slit open an envelope.

'Look,' said the driver. 'Those flats and that marina — Christ, the view. Really great, isn't it?'

'Yes?' I said. 'Um.' Sorting paper. 'Uh-huh.'

Stephen pointed out sights while I went on reading. The turning pages blotted what he was saying, but I realised the car seemed to move around a lot.

'Look,' he said, some time later. 'This is King's Cross. Like Soho — look! Alida? This is famous.'

'Um,' I said. 'Yes. Lovely.'

'It isn't lovely!'

I glanced up at a tawdry, signboard-hung redlight area. Vibrators were advertised as this week's loss leaders and the sex-shops looked the sort to me that give discounts.

'Uh-huh,' I said. 'Not much, is it? I mean, it's *small*, isn't it?' It wasn't half as erotic as the reading matter to hand.

I think that was when Stephen gave up and began driving back.

In the lobby there were new receptionists on duty, and a new voice, very guarded, when I picked up the 'phone.

'Hello, I reported a fault in the air-conditioning.'

'What was that, Madam?'

'I don't have any air.'

'Ah, I really don't know whether anyone's on duty. All I can do is try to get hold of the maintenance man.'

'Couldn't you just send someone up to open my window?'

'No, Madam, we do not open the windows. Please do not *try* to, ah, open your window. It's a hotel rule — security reasons, Madam.'

I studied my letters. The edges were wilting under my thumb. '*What* security reasons? Do you mean suicide? There are easier ways to commit suicide—'

'Yes, Madam—'

'Like suffocation! I may stifle to death here, which will be murder, but I couldn't commit suicide because I've looked at the hinges, and that window couldn't be opened more than THREE INCHES WIDE!'

'Ah, please, Madam, don't try to open the window. Security—'

'Are you afraid of somebody breaking in? Do you think someone's going to climb up twenty-four storeys?'

'Ah—'

'And have the energy left to rape or burgle me?'

'No—'

'If anyone climbed up I'd help them in — it might be mountain rescue with brandy and air!'

A sniff. 'I can only try to get hold of maintenance, Madam.'

'If you don't could you send me up a respirator? Hello?' But the receiver had gone dead.

By the time I met Stephen to go and have dinner, my perspiration was doubling as lip and cheek gloss. After my room, everything was so *cool* – even the main course flambé. It was torture to go back into my fiendish sauna, and the receiver informed me maintenance was out on a job.

'What?' I asked, dripping steadily on the night table. 'Is he working through the building, repairing the windows with bricks?'

I put my laundry in laundry bags, and sweated. Then I sat down, and sweated, and filled in the lists. Then I got up, and hung up my clothes, and sweated. Then I lay down, and sweated, and read my letters. Then I did occupational therapy – and then I *really* sweated. But I didn't mind.

Perhaps if I kept the curtains drawn during the daytime? Then the room mightn't get so unbearably hot.

I got up, and filled in my breakfast order, and sweated. Then I went back to bed, and sweated, and eventually fell asleep.

And next morning, when I was sweating, and eating the wrong breakfast, at the wrong time, in the dark, there came a thunderous knocking and Audrey, the Sydney lady, bounded in – the nub of the distribution complex, the irresistible Jewish mother towards whom I'd been heading ever since I landed. She was just ahead of a housekeeper, who'd come to collect the laundry (that evening a maid would return it – my frilly underwear, pressed and *dry-cleaned*).

Audrey stopped and stared at the drawn curtains. The first words she spoke were a shriek: 'SO WHAT'S WRONG WITH YOU?' A younger, more attractive, English version of Ethel Merman.

I put down my sweaty fork on someone else's breakfast (it became a daily mystery, wondering where *my* breakfast had gone). 'Hello,' I said.

'HELLO,' boomed Audrey. 'WELCOME TO SYDNEY, DARLING. YOU DON'T LIKE LIGHT?'

CHAPTER FIFTEEN

If Audrey was a friendly foghorn, her husband Alex was a double-agent. Bright-eyed and bushy-haired, with a dirty raincoat and a heavy accent, he looked like a pragmatic squirrel who'd just double-crossed the CIA. Alex would have had the chutzpah to send a file in a pork pie to a prisoner of the Israelis, and was probably selling Bibles to the Palestine Liberation Front.

He and Audrey were the heart and head of the distributors network — 'MY FAMILY!' Audrey called the others, conjuring up a Jewish Mafia. From Sydney they dealt with everything, from censorship to employees' ulcers, and now, for a week at least, they had to deal with me. After one meeting Audrey went to a chiropractor; I think it worked out cheaper than a psychiatrist.

Suffering from an excess of concave beds and airline uprights, I envied Audrey the chiropractor but was put into other hands: those of a PR lady, now the schedule was filling up. She was beautiful and efficient, herded me everywhere — and I needed her badly. In TV studios when I wasn't made up she lent me powder and lipstick, she was witty and always punctual and she knew every loo in Sydney. She sat with me in radio stations, in hotel rooms and coffee lounges, she annihilated taxi drivers and actually got me taxi cabs. On foot she rarely used streets, traversing block after block under cover, dragging me into hardware sections and leading me out by some other door. We got about Sydney through gents' outfitters and perfume departments, I was never late for a single appointment and I was never so tired in my life.

Between dates I collapsed and had conversations with the receiver. The topics we discussed offered an ever-new stimulus.

'Hello, could you please tell me what's happened to my laundry?'

'Let's see — yeah, laundry should have left the sixth floor by now.'

'When do you think it'll get to the twenty-fourth storey?'

'Let's see — yeah, about nine or ten o'clock.'

'But you've got my clothes in there and I'm going out at half-past eight!'

A reflective silence.

'Wait — wait a minute. It's supposed to be a same-day service.'

'Yeah. Well, it is, Madam.'

'The same day, not the same night! Same-day usually means it's there when you get back in the evening.'

'Yeah. Well, it will be, Madam.'

And it frequently was. Cellophane-wrapped and dry-cleaned, no matter what my instructions. Personally I prefer my knickers to smell of Madame Rochas. But at least I wasn't as lumbered as the purple-faced man at Reception; collecting my key one day, I heard a suspicious soprano — he was complaining his underpants had been starched.

Perhaps I'd have been better off, taking my woes to Reception, but I couldn't always go down there, not just in a towel.

'Hello? Operator? Could I please have an alarm call, for eight-fifteen in the morning?'

'Sorry, Madam. Alarm calls are only given on the hour and half-hour.'

On the whole, no one could say that the operator and I got on well.

'Hello? Operator? It's very late —'

'Yes, Madam.' Furious night-nurse. 'The time is three

forty-five a.m.'

'Yes, operator, I know, operator, and I want to get some sleep. Could you please put a "do not disturb" note on my number? I don't want any calls put through until I let you know.'

'I understand what a "do not disturb" note means, Madam!'

'Yes, I'm sure—'

'We're familiar here with the procedure, we have visitors from overseas!'

'Of course you—'

'If you don't want to be rung, you won't be rung, Madam!'

'Thank you,' I said humbly, and put a wet towel on my head.

Sometime, somewhere, the mission bells were ringing. I climbed to the 'phone from a deep pit of exhaustion and nausea.

'Hello — just thought I'd call you — haven't changed your mind, have you? Thought not, but you know I'm off to Adelaide.'

This was a voice I knew, though I knew it couldn't be. A lone and very predatory Englishman. A chance acquaintance in Perth who'd dogged me through three cities. I held my eyes open to look, more than crazed, down the 'phone. 'But you said you were off to Adelaide early this morning.'

'Yes, that's right. What a memory. Thought if I called you now you could catch the same 'plane.'

I let my eyes fall shut. Out of the darkness I said, controlledly, 'What is the time, please?'

'I could still pick you up, it's not quite seven o'clock.'

First I put the 'phone down. Then I screamed. Then I lifted the receiver, dialled the operator and said 'Why?'

'What's that?'

'WHY DID YOU PUT THROUGH THAT CALL?'

'Wasn't it for you?'

'Yes, it was for me, but I didn't want it. I asked not to be disturbed, I asked for no calls!'

'Oh, yes, I see. There seems to be some sort of note here. Well, another time you don't need to answer it.'

In that moment I realised why the management feared suicide.

Though why think of only the windows? Why not search guests for sharp objects, and remove their shoelaces and ties?

Sweating, I removed everything voluntarily. I was still in what was obviously Hell's annexe.

'Good evening, it's about the drink I ordered two hours ago. I wouldn't mind, but it's just — you see, the ice-cubes —'

'Yes, right away but it's a busy evening, Madam. We'll try to get to you, Room Service does its best.'

Room Service did its worst with my daily breakfast. It also had temperaments, and had to be soothed. There was a knock at the door while I was on the 'phone one morning, so I called 'I'm coming' and hurried to open up. Framed in the hessian stood a furious mid-European, who must have trained with his trolley in Pamplona, running the bulls. When I got out from under the wheels I heard him screaming: ''ow can hai cumin? Zer doohah iss lock!'

'I didn't say "Come in",' I whimpered. 'I said "Coming".'

'Hah!' He stood and scowled till I'd finished eating someone else's waffles.

When Room Service wasn't careering in with the wrong breakfast, my door was assailed by myriad urgent large fists. Reeling out of bed at some unspeakable hour of the morning, I would be faced by a well-muscled chambermaid.

'Clin yo ruhm?'

'Please could you come back and clean it later.'

'Clin yo ruhm? You hcheckin' howt today?'

'No, I'm not checking out today — I'm not, God help me.'

This dialogue took place daily for seven days.

In the midst of it all I'd escape sometimes, down to the harbour, to sit in that first café where Stephen had taken me. Drink tea and watch the seagulls and tell my cup that I wasn't going mad.

I'd escape with the PR lady, to gossip over platefuls of salad and lobster, watching the little boats bobbing beyond the jetty at Watsons Bay. It was cold now, of course it was, everywhere but in my hotel room. I'd been some time in Sydney so it was currently recording the lowest temperature for eighty years.

And I'd escape to buy chocolate-topped cappuchcino, to spend an afternoon exploring: a ferry to Mosman and one of the crew was wearing a golden earring — wasn't that a little extreme for a quarter-hour ferry ride?

At times like these, outside the hotel, I could almost believe I was sane. I could, moreover, believe that the world was full of sane people. Some of them, indeed, proved to be too sane by half.

There was the glamorous female who interviewed me on her TV show. I'd seen the show already, and marvelled that anyone so fragile could hold together a cluster of guests so inarticulate and *ugly*. Wouldn't it be interesting to meet her. Wouldn't it, if I could've. Up and down gantries, over skeins of cables, from a glassed-in viewing booth above the studio floor — I could see her but shouldn't I meet her? We were briefly introduced before my interview was to be taped. Frowning past me into the battery, she trilled an imperious 'Lippie!' Immediately a dwarf minion sprang out of the cables and painted the exquisite, pouting mouth a darker shade. Since the complexion was already covered in Polyfilla, no further ministrations were considered necessary.

I watched all this fascinated, since none of the guests on the programme had been given even a mirror. And anyway I had no option but to watch: in order to apply the 'lippie' the minion leant right across me, one overalled elbow resting on my bare, shiny face. Under the heat of the lights my lipstick had run into my navel, and whatever had been round my eyes had long since vanished under my chin. The female in Polyfilla flapped her dead mink eyelashes — there she was in the monitor, immaculate and delicate. An assessing glance clawed the air between us. I could see this one was as delicate as a rattlesnake. On went the light, on came her smile . . .

We struck up an instant rapport which was brought to an off-camera conclusion, when she thrust my books at me and said 'D'you want these? Maybe *you* can sell them.'

This is why, I told myself, you have to have a companion. A polite PR lady is with you, if only to pinion your arms. Life for her was far from being all honey. Sitting waiting for my reappearance after a particularly live chat show, she had to listen embarrassedly to two scientists — the next couple on. 'I don't like it,' mourned the husband. 'Having to follow that *dreadful* woman.'

More and more I blessed the every-loo-in-town lady, for Audrey and Alex were busy and Stephen was usually with them. Still, the whole circus wouldn't be in town for much longer now. In a day or two Stephen would be flying onward, and I'd be going my own way because the promotion work ended here. After Sydney I could relax with the Tourist Commission. No more interviews, no more rattlesnakes — just leaning back and enjoying being taken round and shown South Australia.

The Tourist Commission itinerary gave me happy little ripples of anticipation. How helpful and nice he'd been — that man in London — and he'd included every single winery. I'd told him that later I wanted to visit an old school-friend, and we'd both rejoiced that she lived in Adelaide.

'Marvellous. Couldn't be better. Capital city of South Australia. It won't take you any time at all from the Barossa *and* it'll solve the problem of where you go to dry out.'

Sweating in my hotel room, I pored over the papers he'd given me. South Australia wasn't just vineyards — there were these mountains, the Flinders Ranges. And hadn't the London man mentioned some sort of opal mine? I'd get right away from the cities, to where there were windows that opened. At last I'd see the *real* Australia.

Audrey, when I caught her, was . . . well, sceptical.

'YOU WANT TO SEE THE REAL AUSTRALIA? WHY GO OUT IN THE STICKS, DARLING? YOU STAY IN SYDNEY AND COME TO THE CLUBS WITH ALEX AND ME.'

'But surely, Audrey —'

'IT WAS REAL ENOUGH FOR STANLEY MORGAN. YOU KNOW HE WROTE A WHOLE BOOK, DARLING. HE WAS ONLY IN SYDNEY FOUR DAYS.'

'I still think I'd better see South Australia.'

'ALL RIGHT, WHAT CAN IT DO YOU, DARLING? BUT IF YOU WANT TO SEE REAL AUSTRALIA, COME TO THE CLUBS.'

So Audrey and Alex took a mould of the chiropractor and asked me if I had some pocket money and took me off one evening to see the clubs.

I'd seen films of the casinos in Las Vegas, and these pleasure-dome palaces were amateur sets of that. In surroundings that cried out for the Miss World Contest, with eye-bending chrome hung above huge carpet show-rooms, Australians were held up by one-arm bandits and lost large sums of money motionlessly.

I'd seldom seen so much going on without anything happening. The machines whistled and rolled their eyes and spat deafening jackpots, and the people swallowed but were otherwise inert. They remained inert whether they were winning or losing money. Whatever happened to them it'd be right and they needn't move. Women balanced on bar stools with their shopping beside them, one hand supported by a handle and the other by a glass.

Men were propped almost upright, with bloodshot expressions, their knees on the bags of bottles in front of their feet.

'SEE THE BAGS, DARLING? THEY HAVE TO HAVE THOSE BAGS, THAT'S THEIR INSURANCE. IT'S SO TERRIBLE FOR THEM, DARLING, THE LICENSING LAWS HERE. POOR THINGS, THEY CAN'T GET A DRINK AFTER TWO A.M.'

Back in my airless room I thought: Real Australia! Thank Christ for the open spaces, and here I come. Mountains and mines and wine and *open windows.* South Australia, the Barossa Valley – I couldn't wait. Those nice, helpful people who'd meet me, from the Tourist Commission . . . They'd sent me a cable and asked me to ring them up. That was the only question mark – funny, really. When I'd rung they'd said please come to Melbourne and not Adelaide.

Still, I'd looked at the map and Melbourne was very *near* Adelaide. Unless I'd gone and got the scale all wrong again. And the Commission must have very good reasons for asking me to go there. Wasn't it reassuring to know that I'd be in their hands: the responsible hands of those good men selected to represent Australia. Polite, painstaking – just think of the London man.

'What I *can't* get over,' I gushed, very soon to leave Sydney, 'is how *kind* they are – the Australians. And the *men* – they're so *polite.*'

'Oh, yeah, they're polite,' said a redhead, making chimes with the ice in her whisky. 'But they have to be, don't they?'

'Er –'

'They're such bloody awful screws.'

CHAPTER SIXTEEN

The screwing capacity of Melbourne was not to be called in question. That, as the Green-Eyed Monster repeatedly 'phoned to snarl, would be biting the hosts that fed me *and* overdoing by leaps and bounds the trackwork of my research. I should confine myself to hearsay, and subtle questioning of the women. The tone of these instructions left me in little doubt: there'd be no subtlety about the grilling I'd have to go through when I got home.

Questioning of the women? The night before I flew onward, I buttonholed the redhead. Were they really –

'Yeah,' she said. '*Awful.* Up until last year the only time I had orgasms was when I was by myself.'

'*Really*?' I said, excited. 'So we balance each other out! That's the only time I couldn't have them before.' There was an agreeable silence. She drank her Scotch and I drank my brandy. 'Necessity's sort of been the mother of invention. How did you – er – *start* having man-made orgasrns? What happened to you last year?'

'Oh,' she said. 'That's easy. I started doing it with foreigners.'

Subtle questioning of the women? Ever tried being subtle with chapped lips? The question when I landed in frozen Melbourne was not how well the inhabitants managed to do it, but with whom they did it and how they did it at all. In order to penetrate the layers of sheepskin, men would have needed something three feet long, chill-proof and prehensile.

It was bitterly cold, a clear, starry night when I arrived. Christmas weather – if it weren't for the fact that the upside-down Australians usually spend Christmas on the beach. *English* Christmas weather, all frost and cake smells, the air hard to breathe and my fingers dead on the handles of the luggage. The airport and the highway – both of them *English.* Even the mortuary lights strung along to the city reminded me of the years of childhood night-flights, returning to London from the lovely, long Swiss summer holidays, dreading my uniform and the abrupt dusty routine of school.

This was the reverse, though, I thought happily. The work was over and now the real fun could begin.

It was a shock to be proved so totally unclairvoyant. My view of the future was fine, but nobody shared it with me. Up to this moment, I gathered, I'd merely been playing at schedules. When you went on organised sight-seeing, you saw twenty-four sights a day.

And you saw them thanks to the Australian Tourist Commission. The cities now – they glowed with pride – Australia had fantastic cities. Why, right here the architecture –

I waved my itinerary: to me, a relic of the True Cross. *This* was what I'd wanted to do, and why had they asked me to Melbourne?

They looked at each other blankly and then said 'Because *we*'re here.'

Why couldn't I follow the original itinerary?

'Itinerary? Oh, yeah. *The Barossa Valley*? Whoever drew this up . . . Oh, yeah, a South Australian.'

I was to be taken to zoos and art collections and zoos and public buildings and zoos and football matches, and, wasn't I lucky? I might go back to Sydney again.

The sweat of fear dripped down my back and stopped short at the gooseflesh. Not Sydney, oh no, with no air and suicide-proof windows. You might as well be in a zoo . . .

'Can't I see animals anywhere *outside*?'

SYDNEY OPERA HOUSE
PRESENTS
WAGNERS
'JAMES LAST"

'You can see animals outside. We have them in open-air cages.'

Maybe they did in Melbourne, but not in New South Wales. I chewed my lipstick off frantically; it was glued by fresh blood to the chaps. 'I wanted to see South Australia.'

Expansive. A pat or two. There, there. 'You can see South Australia. The Barossa'll take you at most perhaps half a day. We can ring the Adelaide Office – tell 'em you'll go on there some time. They'll fix you up.'

But the big treat was to be a return trip to Sydney, and this time they'd make sure that I did it all properly – the harbour and the clubs and the Opera House. Especially the Opera House, and someone would see about tickets.

I froze to the upholstered polystyrene environmental threat. The Opera House was wonderful, from the outside, but on the inside there was no opera. When I was there I'd rushed to see the programme, and it was nothing but pop concerts for weeks and weeks and weeks. I'd watched the audiences, streaming along the promenade: men, raw-shaved and formal; ladies in long dresses; little girls in velvet and white gloves. At six o'clock in the evening, for a James Last rip-off. English audiences didn't dress up that much for Glyndebourne.

My teeth chattered. 'I've seen so many cities –'

'S'right, but have you seen them *properly*?'

I chewed my chaps, having digested most of the lipstick. How on earth was I going to get out of this? I couldn't say I'd planned to see the real Australia – what was the real Australia, after all? Everyone had their own ideas about real Australia . . . Avoid mentioning the country, they seemed to be shy about that. Called it the bush and made 'let's have a drink' sounds. Suppose I approached my needs from a more oblique angle? 'I'd like to meet an aborigine.'

I was faced across a desk with a set green jelly expression. 'It isn't our policy to introduce *people* to the aborigines.'

Back at the hotel, I sat huddled up in a blanket. Here I could open the window but when I did my tea-pot froze. Oh, God, for an English tea-time. Oh, God, for a voice from England. I telephoned my Mother.

'Ooww! Alida! Are you enjoying yourself?'

I traced round the rim of a saucer. 'The hotel's very comfortable.'

'Ooww, I'm so pleased. I'm so pleased you've got away from that Sydney. Will it be quieter now?'

'Yes . . .' Apart from the trams. She worried so much I couldn't tell her how I was feeling. Or how I was dreading the programme ahead.

We said goodbye, and I sat and looked at my teacup. If I rang Keep The Home Fires Burning I'd have to be more honest, and he might say leave it, and why not pack up and come back.

I pushed away the tea and delved for my old school-friend's number. And the operator said 'You're through — Adelaide.' Through to Jill, with her English accent, and she'd been wondering what had happened to me. The last she'd heard was an air letter mailed from London and the guest room had been tidy ever since. When was I coming, and I said I'd let her know definitely. I put down the 'phone thinking there was a bolt-hole to go to, and if I *had* been clairvoyant I'd have gone on the next 'plane.

For although I foresaw the long week in frozen stiff Melbourne, I didn't foresee the Tourist Commission PR. A gentleman on the staff was a part-time, amateur genius, who handled PR out of fun and sheer lust for life. Not his own life — usually somebody else's. In this case it was unfortunately mine.

Nothing previously experienced could have possibly prepared me — for newspaper, TV and radio interviews, crammed into days already packed with other engagements, and all of it taking place in a freezing city, where the rattling trams and the traffic prohibited sleep. My brain cells turned to ice-cream in the churning onslaught.

'Tell me,' said a TV show host, 'was your husband a good lover?'

'I can't remember!' I wailed, and frighteningly found I couldn't.

'Who's *this*?' quizzed radio show presenters. And I'd read a name and say 'That's the man who sent me.' Then they'd offer me coffee and put on a record, and say 'D'you know he's following you up with press handouts about *himself*?'

Not only that, but his attention was all-consuming. He rang everyone who met or interviewed me, and then he'd ring me to say 'So he's taking you out for a drink!' He rang me so often my long-distance calls didn't reach me, and I actually escaped with thanks to Ballarat.

Ballarat was a must on the interest schedule, because of the gold mining complex at Sovereign Hill. A perfectly accurate little township had been recreated, a walk-round peepshow of life in the first decade after the discovery of gold. Crinolines; leggings; a sweetshop that sold old-fashioned scented sweets; a blacksmith's; the Victoria Theatre, with playbills showing Lola Montes' name; unmade mud streets and the deep and chilly mine.

An earnest young man from the Tourist Commission took me, and drank port to thaw himself and said he'd never known it fine. Whatever the weather was doing in the rest of Australia, in Ballarat it would rain – if it didn't snow.

It rained, and I got very cold and wet. And that night I couldn't sleep in my hotel room. And the next day the world was going round and round. But I had so many appointments, and after the third of them I collapsed having taped a TV show.

In a clinic I was examined by a brisk young doctor. 'Oh,' I bleated, 'I keep *crying* all the time.'

'What have you been doing?' He took my blood-pressure. 'Have you been travelling?' He held my wrist.

'Been here long? Are you here on business?'

'Well —' And I told him what I'd been doing for the past few weeks. Particularly what I'd been doing since arriving in Melbourne.

He went to his desk and sat and thought for a while. Something snapped between his fingers. It was a thermometer. Then he said 'I'd like to see whoever set you up this week go through it. Personally. And your throat — good God.'

'I had my tonsils out a few weeks before I left England.'

'Have you been in much air-conditioning since that time?'

'All the time. In 'planes . . . I get awfully thirsty.'

'When you get back to London I'd like you to see your surgeon. That scar tissue may need tidying up. Your throat's congested — and you're running a fever. Looks like you've caught a dose of Australian 'flu. They've had it in every one of the cities you've been in; I could say you're lucky that you haven't caught it till now.' He stood, and tapped at the pockets of his starched coat. 'Take a taxi back to your hotel — reception here'll call one. And go to bed till tomorrow, and don't try to eat. Tell the operator not to put any calls through to you, and take one of these pills tonight. What you need is sleep. As soon as you feel well enough to travel, get on a 'plane and get out of this whole mess. Is there anyone over here that you can go to?'

'I've got a girl-friend who lives in Adelaide.'

'Keep warm, and ask someone to drive you out to the airport. You'll need help with carrying baggage, and things like that. Go to bed as soon as you can when you get to your girl-friend's, and stay in bed. Rest a lot, nothing heavy to eat.' His hand was on the door-knob.

I said 'How much do I owe you?'

'Nothing, apart from the sleeping pills. That's a small charge.'

It *was* a small charge, far less than the taxi money. I sat behind the Greek driver and cried for the whole of the way.

When I rang Adelaide the guest room was still ready for me. Then I rang Home Fires Burning and he had a long-distance fit. Then I rang my Mother and said I was going to Adelaide, and she said 'You are all right, aren't you?' and I said 'Just tired.'

And then there was a new voice on the 'phone, clear from the lobby. Audrey's local man, coming to the rescue. She'd given me his number in case of just such emergencies, and I'd rung him earlier, very swimmy, from the studio. And best of all, what he had with him was my English publisher, newly arrived in Melbourne on a rush tour. Someone from home! They both arrived in my bedroom, and were duly and indiscriminately wept upon.

'Do you want to go home right now?' Henry asked, over the sobbing.

And I'd have given anything, arms or legs, to have been able to say yes. But still I knew that I hadn't seen the *real* Australia. And to give up now seemed so terribly chicken-hearted. Just because of the cold, and home-sickness, and having the 'flu . . .

Henry handed me a hankie and said 'Don't worry', and another hankie and said 'It'll be all right', and gradually I gave all my worries to him.

And when he and the local man left there were no more 'phone calls, except ones from England that said very comforting things. And I had a bowl of soup and rang a journalist, an English one I'd met who'd been very kind. And he said he'd wrap me in blankets and drive to the airport, and did I need anything and I could quite honestly say no.

I fell asleep without having to hear the PR man, and knowing that there was no schedule to follow next day. Up to my brain in 'flu, doped and very weepy, I cried because I was free and happy, and very relieved. The last words I heard came from the soft television, turned on for company, to lull me gently to sleep.

'Be a sport,' it whispered to me, 'Give blood.'

CHAPTER SEVENTEEN

'Do you have peaches in England? Are you sure you have peaches in England?'

'Yes,' I said restrainedly, 'we do have peaches in England.'

Andy looked at me, disbelieving. 'They're not just what *you* call peaches?'

'They are also what *you* call peaches!'

He cupped his grubby hands round an inflated, imaginary football and said 'They aren't as big as *this.*'

I turned over in bed, but there wasn't as much space as usual — not the acres of sheets that had stretched round me, horribly empty, since I began my Grand Tour of Hotels. I was wrapped up as snugly as in my small bed in the Wendy House. The Wendy House, my bedroom — and I automatically stretched out a hand for the alarm clock that would be caught in a fold of the duvet. My bed is a final resting place for complex supplies of night objects: cassettes for the analgesic tape player, an alarm clock so I can moan in the morning about how little I slept, books and magazines and ear-plugs and my glasses, paper and pens and some paper handkerchiefs. And because there isn't room anywhere for a bedside table, all these things are accommodated in the rumples and slopes of the duvet, between my bulk and the wall. One morning when I was shaking my bedding on the landing, the clock and three tapes and a notebook and my glasses clattered down. Everything was all right, except for the clock, which broke in the basement, and I've tried to winnow my duvet before I shake it ever since.

Where was it? I turned over, with difficulty in the tight blankets, and peered foggily round the room, and gradually realised. I was at my friend Jill's, and it was the crisp, cool early morning, and beyond my door and the dining-room there was a faint rattling in the kitchen — and I was feeling better.

I got up, still very vague about the time. Must find that clock Ben had lent me. From my room, through the dim dining area and cautiously into the kitchen, and there were the boys with cups and plates and shocked, disapproving faces. Ben, whose head reached my knees, said 'Go back to bed, Alida!'

'But —'

'I'm bringing you breakfast in bed so you've got to go back to have it!'

And I dutifully crept away. When I'd drawn the curtains I found the clock and immediately felt very tired. My watch wasn't working any more and Ben had brought me this, a gift for my first night with uncertain legs and a face almost as large as his.

I curled up in bed again, endured the distant crashing and was eventually rewarded by the arrival of a tray. Ben was carrying it sideways.

'You did use my clock? Where'd you put my clock?' he demanded. His head was swivelling madly, his eyes out on tentacles for the hospitably relinquished favourite, the only really grown-up clock he'd once had in his room.

'Yes, it's over —'

And there with a rush and a slither were my slices of toast on the carpet. So charred they seemed to have broken. And they were jammy-side down. I ate them anyway, out of greed and to stop Ben crying, and would find him watching me with curiosity and admiration at odd moments from then on until the end of my stay. That grown-ups were strange, he obviously already knew. That they were strange enough to eat broken toast coated with carpet — that extended the frontiers of knowledge.

My behaviour in general and particularly in the guest room afforded Ben and Andy hours of interest and amusement, not all of it innocent. I performed my exercises, slept at odd hours when I wanted, and bagged Jill's typewriter to catch up on my letters and notes. I also dressed and undressed: Andy found me stark naked and took an extraordinary time to find his way out. Thereafter he followed me closely, and apologised whenever he got the chance.

'It's *all right,* Andy,' I said. 'It was a mistake!' He considered me for a while, concentrating on the hip level, and then went back to his bicycle. 'Yes,' he called, 'it was.'

The gentle, undemanding and cosy atmosphere in Jill's home, the milder climate outside after Melbourne, the English accents, the hours spent turning over old school photographs — 'What d'you think's happened to him?' and 'Didn't he have a crush on her?' — had a fantastically quick remedial effect. Within a few days I was wandering around, still a bit wobbly but by no means so tearful, and even able to drool over the tape Old Home Fires had made me before I left. Since my first few rain-making, heart-rending experiments I hadn't dared touch it, but now I could sit and listen, secure in the knowledge that transportation to the colonies was more than half served.

It was as well my reserves of energy were being so quickly rebuilt. Early one morning there was a telephone call from the man representing the South Australian Tourist Commission.

He was, cripes, he was amazed to find me; he'd been told I'd still be in Sydney; he'd been hoping to get a message to me, he'd been given this address for forwarding, the surname was familiar and it had turned out his wife was in the same choir as my friend.

At the back of my frontal lobes, the alarm bells started clanging. '*What* message?' I said defensively.

It was a chance too good to miss; it would have been

worth flying down for, but I wouldn't have to fly down now, would I? Cripes, I could just –

What did he have on offer, a pavement? But no, it appeared his wife and my friend had had a serious talk. About what I should see in Australia. And he'd managed to contact a man from the Wilpena Pound, up in the Flinders Ranges. Mr Rasheed, the gentleman in question, ran a whole lot of tourist facilities; he was driving up there from Adelaide the following morning and had actually said he'd be pleased to give me a lift. I could stay with him until the following weekend, and have the opportunity to take a real look at the mountains –

'Ah, er . . .' I hesitated, indecisive in the hallway. The memory of the loose knees, tight throat, cerebral fog and terror still fresh in my mind. I wasn't supposed to be doing anything but breathing for at least a week.

'It's the best chance y'll ever get. It's a Hell of a way to the Pound and there's no one else here who c'd drive you.' The South Australian Tourist man coughed, awkwardly, over the 'phone. 'We've only got one car running and I need that to get to work.'

I swallowed. It hurt less than it had done.

'I know you've been crook but the weather up there's usually better'n it is down here.'

So I took a deep breath and said yes.

Jill said she'd been looking forward to having me to herself for a week – her husband had driven off on business and the boys had their bicycles. But – and she lent me a small travelling case and advised me to take only trousers, because as far as she knew there wasn't much up at the Pound. And I packed several pairs of her husband's warm socks, and his old college scarf, and some throat sweets, and my sleeping pills and a medicine chest, and the next day we went to meet the man.

I hadn't been able to appreciate much when Jill had first driven me home from the airport. 'There's the Museum,' she'd said. 'There's the Art Gallery.' And I'd blinked at the floodlit bright darkness, grand Palladian entrances and modern sculpture sliding by.

But now I was feeling better, and the images that had lain flat down on maps rose up like those in a children's book — one where the pages spring out with sets from Snow White or Red Riding Hood. Or the Boyhood of Nelson.

Adelaide was planned by a sailor — a naval gentleman, Colonel Light. And it wasn't a bad effort for his very first attempt. He was appointed Surveyor-General to the Colony of South Australia, and he had to select a site for the capital and draw up a city plan. So he took up his quill pen and did it. And he did it perfectly. In 1836 he designed a lay-out so neat and clean and perfect that every present-day planner should throw up his ruler and search for Light's ghost.

Within one square mile, a city centre of squared-off broad streets, all bisecting at right angles. And one block in from each of the corners of this city centre, Colonel Light set garden squares. Viewed from above, they look like cross-word puzzle blanks.

At the very centre of the cross-word, Colonel Light put another blank square for the sake of pattern. Then he drew a huge border of parkland around the city, and there it was. And there it is. To this day, nearly one hundred and fifty years later, one of the best planned cities in the world. Situated on a narrow coastal plain between Gulf St Vincent and the mountain ranges inland. And I was going to the mountain ranges.

Jill parked near the town office of the Wilpena Pound Reserve and we walked inside. 'Hi, there,' said John Wayne. He wrapped his hand around mine, and my hand vanished up to the elbow.

'Hello,' I said weakly.

'We-ell, we'd better get started. You're ready, are you? It'd be good to get over the driving while it's light. We can stop up at Carrieton, if that's not too long a stretch for you — there's a good watering hole.'

'Oh, yes,' I said. 'Lovely. My throat — I keep drinking

tea.'

He went slightly pale under the walnut and Jill hid her pink confused face.

'Pub!' she hissed at me, recovering.

'What?' I was half through the door with John Wayne. His name he told me, was Kevin, but I preferred to believe the evidence of my own eyes.

'That's what they call a pub — a watering hole!'

'Oh,' I said. 'Goodbye then.' And I went and climbed very nervously into the car.

I regarded the car nervously because of the dent in it. John Wayne gestured at the dent and said philosophically 'Roo'. His voice came from somewhere six feet beneath his shoe soles — a cowboy hero who sounded like Tony Bennett. And was so irresistible kangaroos threw themselves under his wheels? It was already p.m. Not too early to take sleeping pills. But once I was belted in, his philosophical approach rubbed off on me, and I relaxed and supplied him with packs of throat sweets. The croak wasn't normal, he told me: he'd picked up a wog. So I asked him where was the aborigine. But wog turned out to be what I called a bug in England. 'Had this wog for a week or two' didn't mean slavery.

Croaking and chatting, we drove through the outskirts of Adelaide. Into gentle green farmland; and on and on. Open pasture and fresh green rolling country. John Wayne explained the landscape had been thought to be so much like Ireland that the early settlers had christened one part of it Clare.

'But I thought the people who settled here were mainly Germans.'

'Oh, yeah, that's right there were Germans. Lot of German families in the Barossa. But y'see we're a mixture and that's why we've got some strange names. There's the original Abbo names for places, and they've been left as they were plenty of times. Then y'll have some English and some Irish, and in the Barossa it was all German till we had the War. There was a lot of ill-feeling and trouble, and names got changed. Recent years, though, they've started changing 'em back. And haven't y'noticed the Italians around Adelaide?'

Yes, I had. I couldn't avoid them. Near Jill's, the 'Beware of the Dog' signs read 'Attencione Cane'.

The pasture became vineyards, the miles clicked up – one hundred, now nearly two hundred – and the vineyards had gone to leave barren land dotted with scrub. The sun was setting. A sunset I'd never seen before, not even in Technicolor on some auditorium-wide screen. A pale green sky streaked with gold and blood-orange and russet. The mountains we were aiming for spilled ink, with diluted cloud above.

Now ruins began to lean out of the nothing on either side of the dead straight dry road. Fallen, crumbling, the stones without roofs, the frames without windows.– 'They believed the rain'd follow the plough.' John Wayne said thanks very much and borrowed a throat sweet. 'They ploughed the land and they waited.'

'And they waited?'

'And they couldn't wait out the drought.'

The sunset behind the mountains now, a pale gold mount to the Indian ink drawing. Darkness really upon us, and the endless road straight as a Roman way in the car's headlights.

'Orroroo,' he said as the sign bounced past us. 'When I first brought my wife out here, she called it Horroroo.'

Abruptly, in the dense darkness, we came to Carrieton. I don't know what I'd imagined – a market town, somehow, inspired by the name. But Carrieton was a cross-roads, with a pub in the middle, and the cross-roads and the pub were in the middle of nowhere.

I winched myself from my seat, many hours and much thirst since I'd left my mug in the kitchen of Jill's lunchtime home, and we hurried through the cold night into the bar. John Wayne stood me to thaw beside the fire, and introduced me to his son, who was John Wayne Junior, and a beautifully groomed and made-up girl who

ADIDAS
JOGGING
MAKE-UP AND
HAIR DRIER

looked as though she was about to sell me a Revlon lipstick. She was the wife of John Wayne Junior, she helped him run the pub, and they might be in the middle of nowhere but *obviously* she always looked like this.

It was something I couldn't get used to, and it happened whenever I met Australian women. They even made-up perfectly to jog. You'd round a corner and there they'd be, coming towards you. Perfect hair, perfect teeth, perfectly dressed and damply lip-glossed. Jogging off the coffee-morning Pavlova. Driving or having tea or going on a picnic, they always looked as if they'd just got down off a stand.

I looked at Mrs John Wayne Junior and felt dirtier and dirtier. I was more in keeping with the customers.

Along the bar were grouped a band of silent Australians. They appeared to have got out of holes lately, or hibernation, and not to have been in a very good light to dust themselves down.

'Well,' I thought. 'This is it. An outback bar. I shouldn't be here, I don't even drink beer and no one will speak to me.'

At which John Wayne introduced me and every single one of the men stood up and shook hands. First they wiped their own hands on their trousers. Then they each took it in turns to ask if they might buy me a drink. If that happened to me in a bar in England I'd think I must have had a face transplant.

There followed a highly articulate conversation, mainly led by a German who hadn't seen Hamburg for years. *Thirty-five years,* and he has hankering to try and go back. I'd seen it three years before and said what I thought of it, and in the end Mr Wayne dragged me off because I'd have stayed for the night.

I had been too curt in my estimate of the cross-roads: Carrieton was a metropolis compared to the road ahead now. J.W., delayed too long, was in a hurry, and only hit the dirt surface at the top of the humps. His headlights threw pines into nightmares along the roadway, skeleton scrub raised brittle, twiggy fingers and twists of brush crouched and cowered like evil dwarfs. Once a huge pale *thing* loped unhurriedly in front of the bonnet.

'What's *that*?' I shrieked and John Wayne said 'A kangaroo.

'I'm only sorry you're not seeing this in daylight. We're coming up into the mountains and they're quite a sight. Never get over the beauty of it. Never. Just feel so different when I'm getting near to the Pound.'

But although he was sorry he couldn't hold back the darkness, and we hit and dipped and rushed from Carrieton to Cradock, reached and passed Hawker and were back on a bitumen road. Smooth, fast, nearer and nearer, higher and higher, at last the gate and a long, low building – 'Stores,' said John Wayne – and a glitter of lights through the trees – 'Camp site' – and we were drawing up in front of a beautiful building. A swimming pool, lawns, light and warmth striking through vast panes of glass. He drove me round a curving lane to an L-shape, where a row of cabins faced out into shadowy trees. And when we got out of the car and he opened the door for me, it was on to the largest accommodation I'd yet occupied. A carpeted floor ran away from me, for miles, towards the valance of a great wide double bed. Other, long, low day-beds that doubled as couches were to the side along the glass window-wall. Wardrobes, a shower-room, a table and chairs, the heater, a teak cupboard containing all I would need to make tea and coffee . . . When he'd shown me round he left me to wash and change.

I unpacked, and switched on the radio in case I was dreaming, and sat on the vast bed and said 'My God!' and 'My Christ!' and 'Well!'

What on earth had I come to? Mood music and at least seventy-five yards of golden plush curtain. It was a Hollywood set in the back of Bourke.

CHAPTER EIGHTEEN

But not a Hollywood set that discorded with its surroundings. The mellowed colour of the stonework melted and merged in the day, and facing my room as I drew the curtains were the silvery, feathery gum trees.

I walked the paved way under the eaves of the roofing, the air on my face sharp as a knifeblade. This morning I was to have breakfast with Mary, the girl who ran the Motel and lived in her own little prefab house on the mountainside behind the main buildings. I'd met her last night, when I was introduced to all the staff by an expansive Mr Wayne. It had been a sociable evening, to judge by the weight of my head. Good wines in fine glass, silver cutlery and candelabra, the ladies in long dresses — and me in a sweater and trousers, and Jill's husband's borrowed socks. Ah, well, I'd apparently lived up to my image. That's what they'd said in the bar where I met the politician; his PR man had a nose that wiffled, in the way of so many PR men, and he'd written his name on a beer coaster and asked if I needed him.

'Saw you on the Ernie Sigley Show,' he said. 'I thought — that girl's a maniac, unless she's got a script.'

The gum trees lifted like pale hands out of the dewy creek banks, and as I passed them and the cockatoo's cage, the cockatoo called out 'G'day!' Up behind the Motel a mountain rose in slack crumples, the rusty rock edges blunted by time and the weather. Misty weather today. I trudged over paving and gravel, past the office and men working on engines, up steps to a netted front-door and into a little kitchen, and there was Mary telling me that there'd been 'phone calls from Sydney — the switchboard was going crazy, what with my calls to England last night. They hadn't had a telephone at all till a year ago, and long distance was reckoned to be about as far as Hawker.

I sat at the kitchen table, elbows on the lace cloth, sniffing the coffee and toast and the citrus smell of fresh air. Mr Wayne would be joining us later, when he'd seen off the politician, and in the meantime Mary told me how she'd come to be working there. She'd seen the Pound first as a tourist, stayed there as often as possible and eventually been offered a job. For years she had lived in a tiny room tucked away behind the office, taking strip-showers behind screens of blankets, with few possessions and less privacy, but then the prefab house had fallen vacant and she'd been offered it by Mr and Mrs John Wayne. On the understanding that they could have it back if they ever needed it, she had hung paper and decorated and accumulated a cat and a bird and a dog or two. And for people like me, who might feel lonely in the morning dining-room, she made a pot of tea or coffee and talked — in my case, about England. And all those calls. I'd rung Home Fires Burning to let him know that I'd safely arrived, because he'd taken the Adelaide news badly — that I was going away with a man.

'I won't be alone with him.'

Jill, behind in the hall, had said 'Won't you?'

'We won't be alone in the outback.'

'Oh, no!' he'd gritted (I'd heard him grit, distinctly). 'I expect he'll have a few servants along, just to brew the billycan tea!'

And he'd been more right than he knew, in trying to be sarcastic. Everywhere I'd looked there'd been silver and damask, scurrying girls in starched aprons and an obsessive maître d'. It had felt so strange, standing in the cramped office, screaming 'I love you' down the receiver and hearing the echo on the faint line. How could he see it all, surrounded by books and papers, with the English sunshine outside. The cluttered, cold office, and beyond it the long winding corridor that led to the bright dining-room. The glasses and the log-fire and the smiling, burned people, and someone as kind and blunt and paternal as John Wayne at the head of the table, with another of his sons and a pilot, and the restaurant manager and the housekeeper and dark-haired, laughing Mary.

'I love you!'

'What's he like? What's he doing? I don't trust him.'

'I love you!'

'Say it, say it, tell me – I miss you, Christ!'

'I miss you.'

The man Old Home Fires didn't trust was having some back trouble, so I lay on the carpet and showed him an exercise. He still had the wog in his throat too, but I hadn't any sweets left for that. We had more toast and coffee, and I met Mary's pet kangaroo, and then I went off for a walk to the Pound before the weather should worsen. It was cloudy, which was unusual they told me (here we went again) and they wouldn't like me to go and get caught in the rain.

Across the gravel once more, down from the lawns by the Motel and over the stony creek bed, with the store that sold goods to the campers away under pines to my right. I passed the camping site and saw the tents and the anoraked hearties, and teenagers shouting and stamping in the misty cold. Signs everywhere warned against leaving the encampment too late in the day, against leaving it in bad conditions, against leaving it late and alone. The broad track wound between gum trees beside the creek, steadily and very gently up and up towards the rocks. A party of boys in heavy boots clattered past me as I stepped more cautiously, half-walking half-slithering and looking everywhere – at the wispy foliage, at the dappled bark, at the damp slate ridges, at the sawn-off, chilli-con-carne-coloured crags.

Not understanding the name, not understanding why mountains should be called a *Pound,* I'd paged through Jill's reference books in the study that was also my guest room. And there it had been: Wilpena Pound. A huge amphitheatre, a mountain basin, an immense natural fortress, a near-limitless rock dimple — but recognised by the farming pioneers who saw it as resembling a stock-enclosure, so they called it a Pound. And the name stuck. The first newspaper description in 1851 included the words '. . . a very singular locality — a piece of level land capable of depasturing five hundred head of cattle, surrounded by perpendicular rocks which rise to a height of a thousand feet . . . It has been named the Pound.' Wilpena was what the aborigines called it, meaning 'the place of bent fingers', because the formation was so much like a cupped hand.

And the cupped hand rested, palm upwards, in amidst the Flinders Ranges, holding native pines, sugar gums and acacias. It could have been the extraordinary remnant of some prehistoric volcano, but geologists dismiss it as an undulation of the sandstones that form the summits of all the higher peaks. Not very romantic, geologists. An undulation, indeed.

I sat on a slab of rock, struggling with my breathing. If this was an undulation, the Empire State Building was a deep hole.

A brief shaft of sun struck on my face, but it was the exertion that had warmed me. The air was thin in my labouring lungs, like a cool damp web of spun ice. From here and there in dips and trees I heard boots scraping, and voices. The clouds had hazed over the rim of the Pound and echoes sprang up and back. As far as I could see, though, not a sight of people. And gradually the people-noise faded and left only rustling and the branches' creak. I tilted my head back, awkward in thick scarves and sweaters, and stared at the broken red ridges and the climbing, clambering green. And smelled the smell that is a pain to city noses — the smell of undiluted air, without additives or artificial colouring or monosodium glutamate.

At lunch I would have been quiet, if the call hadn't come through from Sydney. A newspaper wanted to interview me, and were doing it now by 'phone.

'You're *where*?' shrilled someone. 'Where the Hell's *Wilpena*?'

'It's in the Flinders Ranges,' I said.

'Yeah, but where the Hell's that?'

'They don't know,' I said, returning to Mary. Beyond her living-room windows the gum trees leaned and led up to the Pound. I couldn't stop looking at it – its colouring changed with every cloud movement – and Mary grinned at me, kindly, and said 'I never get tired of it either.' And then she said 'No, they don't know.'

CHAPTER NINETEEN

Perhaps I'd have got to the mosquito before he got to my jugular. Anything might have happened, if I hadn't had quite so much to drink.

I'd fallen in bed, and yes I'd heard this buzzing, but then I'd thought so what. So what I'd thought, and hiccuped. It must be just a housefly.

There was mosquito netting everywhere, all over all of the windows, and a huge garden-size can of deadly mosquito spray. It sat on top of my 'fridge, looking aggressive. But that, I was sure (and hiccuped) was for the summer. For the hot weather. I slid into sleep, sloppily, and hiccuped. Whoever heard of mosquitos in winter?

Except that it wasn't winter when I woke up: the sun was already blazing on the gum trees outside my door. I went to wash my heavy, hung-over face in the bathroom, and shrieked and leapt back at the tiles when I'd seen what I saw.

Running down from one ear like the work of a bloodlet of vampires, mountainous lumps distorted my cheek, neck and jaw. I touched one of them, horrified, with a finger, and it immediately set up a pulse-beat, an itch and a throb. It even glowed slightly. Not to be outdone, its example was followed instantly by all of the others. Jibbering, I soused myself in calamine. Now there appeared in the mirror a hung-over, lumpy dalmatian. I looked on the bright side and winced. The calamine did *nothing,* absolutely nothing for the maddening itch but at least it would tell the world what I had was bites. I couldn't have borne to be thought the victim of some vile English disease.

'We-ell, now, what has happened to you? Y'poor little thing.' Mr Wayne took my hand in his paw and examined bits of me closely. My overnight guest had also had a long gnaw at my arm. 'Didn't y'use y'spray?' His voice sounded better today; with the sunshine his wog had flown.

'I thought there wouldn't be any mosquitos in winter.'

'Up here y'have to be careful. We've always got the little buggers. But they don't really bother y'unless y've got that fair skin.'

I had that fair skin all right, a whole 5′7½″ body of it, and presently I was thanking God for my voluminous Victorian nightdress. Chaste down under, I'd eschewed silk nighties and French knickers and wrapped myself up at nights like an impenetrable parcel for Oxfam. At least the vampires had been foiled in the delicate area between my elbows and neck.

Trying to keep my long fingernails away from the furious itching, I cursed all insects and bewailed that today of all days – for I was being taken on a long drive through the Ranges, the sky was cobalt, the sun brilliant, all I'd wanted to do was to look and take photos – and now all I wanted to do was scratch. I grimaced at J.W. and he slapped the wheel, and the car swung away from the Motel. We were in convoy for part of the way with another party: two couples there with a driver who looked like Clint Eastwood, and we were all to meet up for lunch.

The bitumen road was soon left behind for dust roads which twirled and wound as we sped from Wilpena. There were shoulders and brows and elm trees, and signs by dry creek-beds with warnings writ large of flash-floods. We passed waving, narrow-eyed Rangers, their trucks full of green-bagged rubbish; and metal signs cut out in dog-shapes to overawe sheep.

The mountains rolled and gathered themselves around

us, purple, red, chocolate, in folds overgrown by green, and the ground swelled and subsided beneath the car wheels. On either side, at every moment, were changes. And above us the eagles, perching and flying, their wing-spans easily six feet. Now the scenery from *Stagecoach,* now the Grand Canyon, now Wales, now the Fjords. We stopped frequently, whenever we saw the other car with its snapping occupants. Photographs of vistas, photographs of gorges, photographs of large ladies in trousers and beads. Photographs of a flight of birds, and a notice that read Bunyeroo Valley. And again the road, and again the winding, and John Wayne telling me how they'd filmed a stunt here for a car commercial and he'd never taken such risks in his life. 'We-ell, not that many times in a couple'hours.'

Again a pause, and the drivers consulted, and chose a shady creek bank for a barbecue. We gathered dry bark to make a fire, and I used it to slap at my bites. From everywhere now more mosquitos dived upon me, as vicious as airborne piranhas, hungry and scenting fresh blood. I slapped like a maddened flagellant, but they seemed to like it. Perhaps they were masochists. I performed a little dance, not elegant but vigorous, and the rest of the party stopped collecting bark, and collected around me to watch. Then I had another slap, and a weep, and people said 'Oh dear' and someone suggested the fire. So I stood in the smoke like a would-be minstrel, hoping to be cooked rather than eaten alive, and Clint Eastwood stoically looked the other way and barbecued steaks and chops. Expertly, neatly, he turned the sausages on a large square of metal balanced on some oddments of rock. The smell of raw meat gave place to the smell of burning, but the flies knew it wasn't me. The aroma merely aroused them further. John Wayne shook a great paw at me and said 'Y'poor little thing' and offered me real billy tea. It was pitch black, intolerably sweet and milkless, and I looked upon it with as much favour as the little girl looks on Corn Dodgers when they're offered to

JOAN OF ARC?

her in *True Grit.* Thank God there were also more civilised beverages, provided in assorted cans. Under the baking sun my throat crazed me from the inside with dryness and from the outside with incessant itching, so I opened can after can and drank.

Which led to another problem. One in which, for once, I wasn't alone. A large lady in beads approached me. 'Heh-hrrm,' she choked delicately. 'Er – we are going up *there* for a little *walk.*' She pursed her lips and looked childish.

Now, I knew what she meant. If I didn't go for a walk soon something childish would happen to *me.* But something adult would happen if I took down my trousers. I would be bitten, *there,* by the mosquitos, who knew neither mercy nor shame.

This impasse bothered me until it was almost too late to be bothered, but then I solved it – inspiration born of desperation – by having another go at the smoke. Filching a cigarette from Clint Eastwood, I disappeared to unzip my trousers for as short a time as was humanly possible, and puff frenziedly behind the trees. It seemed to work. I had no more bites in that tender region. Just the hundred or two that I already had covering my neck and my arms.

The ladies having attended thus coyly to their bladders, we re-entered the cars and then got out again and briskly fanned the seats. Then we all got in again and revved up the dust on the dirt road, and they disappeared round a crag-face and our car spun onwards to Fossil Rock.

The Flinders Ranges are so old only God can have created them, and the area around Fossil Rock is just that – nothing but fossils. Huge clumps, broken blocks, scattered pebbles. It's merely a question of taking the ones you can carry, and remembering my air luggage I sought out little ones. A large chunk, though, for Jill and her family, with two small ones for me, their surfaces veined with the worm loops and round homes of ancient animals. I sat in the car looking at them, wetting them with spit to see their make-up more clearly.

'Good'uns, huh?' asked John Wayne.

'Yes, very good. Very.'

On and on, through a gorge and out into the plain now, where the heat struck up and the sun struck down and burned my arm as it rested on the wide open window. And this in the so-called winter. My bites rose and throbbed unbearably as the temperature increased. We were driving along beside a stretch of the old Alice Springs railway, the blue metal sky above, nothing off to the West but the flatness and the Ranges to the East, on our right.

At Parachilna, a little railway halt, we stopped. There was a pub, and an outhouse. And the outhouse made me glad I'd used a cigarette under the trees. I poured brandy down my throat, and ice-cubes, and touched my reddened wounds with the cold glass, and prayed for the itching to stop. The gnarled elderly ladies who ran the pub were pleasant, and welcoming, and I stopped praying about my bites for a moment to wonder about their life. Outside the bar, as far as I could see, was nothing. Nothing except a few buildings and a Rock Shop. What did they do, in the midst of this aridity? Try to foster a garden, by the look of it. A garden and a pub and an outhouse, and women in this waste. What could Parachilna have been like when it was the railway station to which all the copper was brought from the most productive mine in the Flinders? Had it been a lively, busy place? It didn't look as though it could ever have been that. Surely the weight of the heat must have stifled all life, must have weighed down and depressed any and every excited movement, every brainwave.

We piled in the car again, and John Wayne drove on to Blinman. And now at last the sun was leadenly descending. Another pub in the quaint mainstreet of this eerie ghost-town. We earmarked it and drove on to the mine: closed in by high fencing, for safety and sightseers' sake. This, with its derelict workings, was once a fantastic source of wealth. Jill had found the piece about it. Discovered by a shepherd called Pegleg Blinman, who went down to posterity with a newspaper report from the 1860s:

'Mr Blinman, the discoverer of the great Wheal Blinman Mine, had his leg broken here the other day caused by a stump in the road. He is doing as well as can be expected. Had it broken below the knee the services of a medical man would not have been required, as in that case a carpenter would have repaired the fracture — it being a wooden leg as high as the knee joint.'

Blinman had once had a population of two thousand. Its population was now ten. I picked up a tiny stone by the high fencing, and it showed viridian in the dimming sunlight.

'That's right,' said John Wayne. 'Copper.'

Too much copper killed Blinman, he said, and then too little of it. Copper found and mined all over Australia, copper in a glut and then a surplus, that made a nonsense and then a nothing of the price. There were a few writhings, money was poured into plant and machinery, the town had bursts of new life but then it finally died about the end of the First World War.

The caved-in shaft, the slag dump — I scratched and John Wayne stopped me, and said 'Let's go for a drink.'

Here, at this pub, I thought, there will be a decent bathroom. It once had a population; it still had questing tourists. And I was covered in dust and blood. I excused myself from the bar and ran upstairs to the ladies, and there in one of the cubicles I found a very tall man. At least, I imagined he was tall since there seemed an awful lot of him. He was projecting out, legwise, towards the mirrors and incidentally mending a lavatory.

'Just in case you're working on all of them,' I told him, 'please don't move on till I come out. I'll be in this one, here.'

'OK.' His voice was muffled. Then he said 'Be my guest.'

When I emerged I had a good wash and held cold water next to the pulse-beats, and I saw the man watching me, curious, in the mirrors. 'Mosquitos,' I explained, wriggling. 'The itching's driving me mad.'

'Mosquitos!' And with that the man unfurled himself like an unfolding sectioned ruler and stood up to his considerable height. He looked extremely commanding, so I followed when he said 'Come with me.'

We hurried along the passage, him striding and me trotting to keep up, and ducked into his little room. And life a conjuror, from his plumber's bag he produced a can of spray. 'It's a *personal* insect-repellent,' he said, very earnest. 'And *that*'ll keep 'em off you.'

It was a brand new can and he wouldn't accept any payment. He just sat on his bed spraying me and asking about England, and then he went back to his lavatories and I went down to the bar. There was a man there in a big hat and boots with a horse missing, and I showed him and John Wayne my present, and he said 'Mosquitos!' just like the man in the lavatory.

'Mosquitos!' He drank his beer slowly. 'Round here they've got fangs the size of bull's horns and we have 'em mounted and hang 'em on walls.'

Driving back to Wilpena, I stared as the sun sank behind the purple ranges. We passed an airstrip, and J.W. pointed out the grazing kangaroos. He drove the car, bouncing, up closer to them — large males, small babies, loping away suddenly — but after all not sudden because they seemed to rise slowly and effortlessly.

The trees stood between us and the sunset, one bare one so draped with pink-white birds it looked as though it were in flower. I glanced at John Wayne, a question, and he said 'The birds? They're galas.'

'Oh, stop!' I grabbed his arm. 'Please stop, please stop!'

The sun had made a golden rim of the purple-black

ridge, a single tree was caught in the molten light as though it had been pinned – I clambered from the car, balanced the small, cheap camera on the roof and took a picture. 'I just wanted –' I said, and then stopped. Taking a picture was stupid; it could never match the subtlety of the light and the wild, dry smell of the evening. 'I just wanted to take a photograph of the real Australia.'

CHAPTER TWENTY

'You could have it set for an engagement ring,' someone said, over the opal. It glowed, pink and gold fires in a midnight, on the little soft mat on the bar. John Wayne had an album of opals, and I was paging through it, hovering over this one and that one. I was also, as usual in that atmosphere, more than slightly the worse for wear.

Running feet had come pounding along the cabin catwalk, and cries of 'A call from England!' had dragged me half-dressed from my room. Home Fires, envisaging me in some romantic, lone mountain eyrie, had thrown caution to the winds with his bank book and was ringing me to hear those vital words that are other people's clichés. He also proposed; it was a habit. His delightful proposals had followed me from England through the previous four States of Australia and were no less pleasant to hear now, in the fifth. Interesting, how my reaction to his proposals had changed. Back home in London I'd been very calm about it, and had said yes, I'd love to live with him but I didn't *ever* want to get married again. The flat-on-my-back flight to Singapore, the week on the boat with the buggers, the sodden arrival in Perth had combined and turned me into a quivering, spineless feminine jelly. The first words I'd uttered to him over the 'phone had been 'Yes, I will marry you, *please.*'

And this evening, up here in the mountains, I'd found my way from the office and been greeted in the dining-room with 'Another call from England? Was it him?'

'Yes,' I'd said, still overcome by the clichés. 'He wanted

to 'phone to propose.' The rest of the sentence, in which I went on to explain that it was for the umpteenth time of asking (and for the umpteenth time of saying yes) was drowned in the general uproar, and Australian calls for champagne. Congratulations reared round me, I blushed and revelled in them, and now I was here in the bar, being shown the album of opals.

''ll get the boys to fly y'to Andamooka!' John Wayne was as jubilant as an old-fashioned father. 'Show y'a real opal mine!'

Still toasting from the hot weather, still full of the sights of the day, my ears overflowing with long-distance love and near-at-hand congratulation, I said oh how thrilling, and scratched.

It was disappointing the following morning that the weather was overcast. Particularly as the lowered temperature didn't alleviate the itching. I covered myself in calamine and was looked at askance and driven out to the 'plane by the Wilpena-based one of John Wayne's sons. He and the young, dark co-pilot sat in the cockpit chatting and I sat behind them, finding ominous sick-bags in the back of their seats. I had never taken off from a dirt airstrip like this one, and it was over ten years since I'd been in a light 'plane. Disquieting memories flickered in me as we jolted over the rough surface. I remembered flying through a hail-storm, and hearing the two pilots saying to one another 'Where are the parachutes?' and 'What d'you mean where are the parachutes? That's the Thames down there, we couldn't bail out.'

We hit a large lump of something which had come out of a kangaroo. And how I longed for suspension. Thank God, *thank God,* we'd soon be up in that smooth air.

With a lurch, with a hitch, with a big-dipper sensation, we were up in the air at last and it wasn't smooth at all.

For those who have never flown over a mountain range in a small 'plane, I would suggest that they don't. I held on to the arm-rests so tightly my fingerprints are still there. Embedded. When that aeroplane is dismantled,

TEST YOUR GRIP!
SHOCKED
SCARED
AGITATED
JEE-ZUS

those prints'll be the last things to go.

We staggered, we pitched, we went down in a bottomless lift shaft and then again we soared up it. And all the time the two chaps sitting in front of me had a relaxed conversation and talked over the radio to Hawker. I'd brought barley sugar, in case my throat began troubling me, and for something to take my mind off things I stuffed the whole packet in my mouth. I was so frightened I wasn't even itching. Occasionally one of the boys would turn and shout over the racket of the wind and the engine to attract my attention to some point of interest, but everywhere I looked the peaks were going up and down.

'Yes,' I said tautly. 'Beautiful. Yes, I see. St Mary's. Oh, really. Mount Rupert. Ooooh-oh.'

'Gets more boring —' His voice was torn away and powdered by the noise.

'What?'

'Gets more boring — out over the Salt Lake. Just patterns —'

Just patterns, but smooth. Beyond the mountain range the aeroplane steadied, the green cloud-covered peak walls pulled back behind us and ahead the dust plain stretched till it was lapped by the Torrens Salt Lake. I took my fingers out of the rests and craned beside the window, my seat-belt cutting deeply into my waist. Below us the railway from yesterday, etching from Brachina to Parachilna, past Leigh Creek and Lyndhurst, towards the Centre and Alice Springs. What were the old ladies doing in their pub today? Moving slowly, opening cans and moving slowly, exactly as they had been doing yesterday? The only difference was the date and the rainy weather. Would the rain make their garden grow? Perhaps a little. Probably it would take much more than this. There was just a light spatter, beads made into odd shapes across my window by the force of the 'plane's flight.

Beneath us now began the marble — flat pools of

spilled milk lying in modern-art arrangements on the warmth of the red sand. Blue and grey veins and hazing. The light muted by cloud, softening and blurring the colours until they seemed to ripple like the water of a real, live and moving lake. I forgot the bounce, I forgot the returned itching, I stopped sucking the barley sugar and sat and stared. I didn't take any pictures, though the boys turned and obligingly pointed out good aspects and welcome tricks of sudden, piercing light. The Salt Lake hypnotised me, its flat loops opening and closing, its white in circles transparent and then in circles opaque. I sat with my face against the cold window, with the traces of moisture forming tracks between me and the beauty for a very long time, I know. We were flying North and slightly Westward, up the length of the lake, to the opal field just West of its Northern tip.

'There it is,' said one of the boys, and I stopped looking sideways and downwards, and started looking ahead. No more marble beauty, but deadly brown earth, and ant-hills. That was what they looked like, white and off-white circular humps. Holes in each of their middles — no, not ant-hills, volcanoes — and, as we circled lower, a fragile shanty town. A drive-in cinema, its screen reared up over nothing. A forlorn little church. A collection of tin roofs and shacks. This was *opal mining,* and consider what opals were worth. I boggled down at it, as we fell nearer and nearer. It got no better as we got closer: lean-tos of galvanised iron, stone and brick and bits of abandoned cars. *Hens*? We landed perfectly on rather a lot of dirt. I climbed out and started scratching and the pilot shook his head at me.

'I never seen,' he said, 'that many bites in me life.'

'You ought to thank me,' I spat. 'If it hadn't been for me, look what you'd have missed!'

A car that had suffered from something, and badly, was churning towards us. Its driver was introduced as Rudi, pumped my wrist and jounced us on our way.

''ll go and have something to eat' – and we rattled and shook our livers to Rudi's guest-house, a cafe with plastic tablecloths and a Woolworth's cruet, and a fortune in opals kept in the house behind.

'What do they do here?' I asked the boys.

'Make money.'

'Yes, but what else do they do?'

'Get drunk.'

They not being Rudi and his wife, but their clients. Rudi and his wife were busy in their time. Inga produced food for Napoleon's army, and Rudi showed me round his bottle house. It was a curious structure, at the end of his transport cafe, built to resemble a stubby beer bottle in shape. Even more curious, it was built *of* stubby beer bottles, emptied with joy and cemented together with care. When you stood inside, you were centralised in a beehive, and you gazed out through the round cells of dark amber glass.

'How many bottles?' I gaped.

Rudi twitched his trousers, twitched his nose and said 'Hundreds.' The bottle house was more than two storeys high. In Andamooka, a clutch of flimsy one-storeys, it was a building really worthy of remark.

We sat over coffee and looked at our plates and some opals, and I asked again, incredulous, 'What do they *do*?'

Rudi and Inga shrugged. She said 'Make money.'

'There's more to life than money!' No one believed me. 'How the Hell can anyone spend their life here?' They looked at the plastic cloth, then out of the window. It was coming on more heavily to rain. 'You told me even *water's* brought in by tanker.'

'Hoh, it's not water they're worried about.' Rudi eased his belt and leaned on the table. 'Look, I tell you the sort of thing happens all the time here. We had that chap – d'yer remember?' The boys remembered. 'That one went and blew up the GPO? Put a call through to his girl and she said they was finished. He blew up the 'phone with the dynamite he had from his mine. He didn't care the 'phone box was on the Post Office. Coulda killed somebody, he wasn't careful.'

Everyone nodded. I swallowed my coffee, and choked.

'Then we had that call one night — d'yer remember, Inga?' Inga remembered. 'Friend of ours, terrified, some bloke was trying to break in her house. She could hear shouting and cursing and breaking up the verandah. Well, don't I get in my car and go there? And there's this dead-drunk feller, tells me to get off, he's only smashing up his own house. I told him it wasn't his house, he broke me teeth before he'd believe me. He was so drunk he'd lost himself going back home. Couldn't make his key fit, banged on the door but she wouldn't open it, so he thought his wife had got a new bloke and they were in there with him locked out. So he started smashing the place up. Oh, he was sorry the next morning. Went and mended the whole verandah.'

I had another choke and a scratch.

Rudi looked at me sorrowfully. 'D'yer know, I never seen that many bites on one girl in my whole life.'

We'd been going to spend the afternoon at Andamooka, but for some reason the boys began making moves towards home. They were casual about it, but then they were casual about everything. They could have been bored, or tired, or homesick, or there could have been a fire. They stared quite a lot at the sky.

I didn't mind, my day had been made by the Salt Lake. I would be very happy to have another look at that.

The car bounced us back towards the airstrip, making a short detour in and out of the mines. White ant-heaps, being scraped at by earth-movers. I itched, and clawed myself. To think that beautiful opals could come out of ugly old *that*.

The rain patted my face as I scrambled into the aircraft — not really heavy rain, though the clouds were much heavier.

'Like to sit in the front? Y'll get a better view this time.'

We seemed to lift very quickly away from the red dust, and the off-white mounds and the beat shape of Rudi's square car. Andamooka dwindled, was lost to the Salt Lake, and I settled to my happy, transfixed musing. The boy who'd flown us out was dozing in the back. Rippling patterns, white and chocolate and grey merging – the time passed, the chap behind me snored. When I grew sleepy I studied the pilot's profile.

He tapped his ear-phones and frowned slightly. 'Hey, they're saying they're waterlogged at Wilpena.'

The bloke in the back woke up and said 'Oh, yeah?' and 'Try and raise Hawker.'

'Seem to think it's pretty heavy at Hawker.'

'Oh, yeah?'

We sat in silence for a while. It came to me that beyond us I could see nothing. The mountain range was hidden in banks of sodden cloud. I twisted in my seat. Behind us I could see nothing. I turned back. Grey mass upon grey mass. The windscreen was trailed with necklaces of whipped rain.

The boys began having a discussion. It had to do with following the road.

'Do you mean,' I asked faintly, 'you can't see where we are going?'

The pilot regarded me strangely, and then he said 'Can you?'

Every one of my bites stopped itching. They'd been struck dead by fear.

'Now, if we can't use Hawker . . .' The bloke in the back blinked. 'Leigh Creek?'

Leigh Creek responded cheerfully. I could hear the derisive laughter. They also had water, and mud.

'D'they think it'll clear at Wilpena?'

'Yeah, it could clear at Wilpena.'

'Try it. We could always turn round – spend the night at Andamooka.'

'No!' Since the stupid question about not seeing where we were going, I had been quiet, apart from my heart.

'No, no, we can't go back.'

'Why not?' asked the pilot. 'S'comfortable at Rudi's.'

'I want to go on to Wilpena.'

'*We* want to go on to Wilpena, but we may have to go back. To Andamooka.' It hurt him, visibly, talking to a Pom who was as silly as a wheel.

'We can't spend the night at Andamooka!'

'*Why not?*'

'Because my mascara's at Wilpena, and so is my calamine!'

They talked to themselves after that.

This time I didn't even notice the bucketing. We were over the range, in the range, were we? No, flying along beside it. Peaks loomed and faded, cloud cleared and gathered, I watched the elongated drops on the windows and held tight to the clasp on my belt. Up and down, dragged and lifted, the boys' voices quiet and gentle, constant on the radio. Hawker — no, not Hawker. Leigh Creek better, but not Leigh Creek. Wilpena — no, try Hawker. And Hawker was clearing up.

We slid down out of the greyness and jolted to a stop on the airstrip. The shortest, quickest landing I'd ever had. Rain was torrential, pelting all around us: it rebounded a foot high off the wing. I clambered out of the aircraft and my feet disappeared beneath me. The 'plane was up to the wheel-hubs in bright red liquid mud. And there was a figure, waving and beckoning from the roadway, hurrying towards us, half-frowning, half-grinning with relief. John Wayne, picking me up and bundling me through the downpour into the car.

'I thought you were driving down to Adelaide,' I panted, wiping my face, smearing my eye-shadow.

'Yeah, half-way down when I just had a thought to ring back. Heard what was happening to the weather before y'left Andamooka.' He patted my wrist, he gripped at the steering-wheel. I remembered the airstrip, I remembered that one of the boys was one of his sons. He tilted his chin at the little aeroplane as the blokes fussed round it, cheerful and soaking. 'We-ell, that'll be bogged in there for a week.'

That night I bought the midnight-blue opal with the aurora borealis glittering from its strange depths. We all had an awful lot to drink — even more than we had to drink after my umpteenth proposal. Somehow there seemed an awful lot to celebrate.

CHAPTER TWENTY-ONE

'Who took these out?'

I tried to answer but couldn't: my mouth was full of his torch.

'Didyer have it done by a doctor?'

There was a crunch as I bit on the bulb part. 'Of course I had it done by a doctor!'

'Hrrm.' He snatched his torch away and used it to cut a cigar. 'Don't like the look of that scar tissue.'

'I don't like the feel of it, much.' I was back in Adelaide. With a memento. I'd got John Wayne's wog.

'Didyer have 'em taken out by a surgeon?'

'I had my tonsils taken out in one of England's best hospitals! My throat was *quite all right* till I got over here.'

'How long yer been over here then?'

'It must be about six weeks.'

'That'd be about it. Yer aint got no anti-bodies.'

'What? I beg your pardon?'

'Yer aint got no anti-bodies. It's a whole new world here. Yer might as well be on the moon. Yer aint got no protection — it's a whole new lot o'wogs. Come down with everythin' goin'. See it all the time with migrants.'

'I am not a migrant.'

'Hrrm. Well.' He looked disapprovingly at his cigar-end. 'Take one of these four times a day.'

So I took to the guest-room bed again, and spread the wog round the younger, more gregarious members of the family, and Jill answered the telephone for me, and one evening I was allowed to baby-sit and rub the boys' chests in with Vick. I was just about at the ambulant stage when Jill called me to the 'phone one morning: it was a TV Channel confirming the time they'd be sending the car.

'Look, I'm sorry —' I swallowed the lemon and honey. Wherever I went now I had a mugful of lemon and honey. That saved me writing the notes. 'I'm sorry, I don't understand.'

'You did a show for our Channel in Sydney. You did a show for our Channel in Melbourne. That's when we booked you, you said you were coming to Adelaide.'

'Oh, my God.' After Melbourne I had forgotten. I had completely forgotten. And there I was in Jill's housecoat, with the honey and lemon and Brian's socks, with a phial full of antibiotics and a throatful of John Wayne's wog. 'When are you sending the car?'

'Tomorrow morning at nine o'clock.'

I put down the telephone and found Jill looking at me. She raised an eyebrow and said 'How many lemons can you eat?'

The 'phone rang again. I hadn't moved so I was nearest to it, and I answered it. The unmistakable *joie de vivre* of the South Australian Tourist Commission.

'Hey, you're back!'

'Yes, but —'

'Bet you enjoyed Wilpena. Hey, this c'dn't be better. Real great the way it's worked out. You wouldn't believe the chance —'

'Oh, no.'

'What was that?'

'Nothing.'

'The people at Kaiser Stuhl'd like to host you — show you all around the Barossa Valley. I c'n pick you up and drive you down there.'

'But I thought you said you only had one car.'

'Yeah. But for something like this — you ever tasted that Red Ribbon Shiraz?'

I drained my mug and husked 'When will you be

driving me down there?' and Jill went silently out to the garden and picked every lemon she had.

'Pretty way out to the Barossa, isnit? Called the Chain of Ponds.'

For some time now I'd been spared a certain brand of Australian driving, but the South Australian Tourist Commission man was making up for all that. I slithered along the seat till I met the gear lever. Ah, well, I thought, settling back. Things could be worse.

'Pity we haven't gota lota time.'

I was flung away and cannoned into the door. What it would have been like without a seat-belt I couldn't imagine. This was as bad as flying to Andamooka — and there'd been some excuse then: the 'plane had been up in the air. Mind you, the car was having a go at that.

'Try to get out to the Barossa wheneverits possible. Great out there. I go every chance I get.' Without moving, he jabbed me in the ribs with an elbow. My ribs had swung near his elbow at the time. 'Wait till you taste it. You just wait till you taste it.' I shot him a paralysing look from where I was hanging on the door-frame. 'That Spaetlese! That port! That claret! Didya know the Queen visited Kaiser Stuhl?'

'Did she — ooohoh!'

'Hah, great road, isnit?'

I disconnected myself, regretfully, from the gear lever, and straightened my clothes and said 'Did they bring her out this way?'

'Nice route, isnit? We'll be passing the stud farm where they gave her a horse.'

'Re — whoops — eally?'

'Hey, was that your —'

'Yes, but don't worry.'

The S.A.T.C. man suddenly looked like Andy. 'Yeah,' he said, and rubbed his nose. 'It was an accident.'

We had ricocheted round a series of reservoirs and gulleys, beneath pine-covered slopes and out into a valley, half the time with me half out of the car, the rest with us both in the driver's seat. It seemed a rather informal way to be visiting somewhere important — a settlement of such significance in the history of Australia. As we drove under the archway spanning the road at Lyndoch, with the legend 'Barossa Valley' written up above us in ornate script, I told myself I was feeling impressed and with luck I wouldn't be car-sick. Where we were going was *famous.* There were people here who still spoke German, in dialects handed down. The churches they had built were old, and the vineyards, and the habits. They'd probably greeted the Queen by singing Lutheran hymns. Hills, funny old high-streets, inspiring monuments flashed past.

And then in a flash they weren't flashing, and the thirsty S.A.T.C. man drew up in a seizure of brakes.

We were stationary, if not parked, in front of a curious building: a cross between a brewery, a manor-house and a château. The brick-work was old-rose in colour, with pale deckled flutings and edgings. There were two rather heavy-set turrets and double front steps to a large portico.

'Thisit,' said the S.A.T.C. man, bounding ahead of me. I followed him inside more sedately, and was never quite the same, or so sedate, again.

Perhaps it was going back to the claret, twice, after the champagne and the rosé. Or perhaps it was going back to the champagne and starting all over again.

Perhaps it was having the three different wines with lunch, or maybe it was the port afterwards. Or then again maybe it wasn't. Because I'm told I said 'Good evening' to the people I met before lunch. And then went and sat down in a chair without actually bending my legs.

Perhaps it was the staggering (and I do mean staggering) hospitality extended everywhere in the Valley, not only by my kind hosts but by the owners of the other wineries that I was taken to see.

Perhaps it was the vineyards that made the wine even more alluring.

All I know is, I was there but I don't remember it very much. And I made notes but I can't read them. I couldn't read them the day after I'd written them. I got back to Adelaide with a severe headache and an awful lot of bottles, and one of those corkscrews that will get you out of whatever sort of trouble you may find yourself in.

Several days had passed, I gathered, of which I could recall nothing clearly after the mornings.

But luckily it had still been a.m. when I met Mr Schiller It was the one and only bright, warm morning in a sullen week of icy wind and rain. To me, of course, the weather had scarcely mattered, because I'd kept my chin up on champagne. But that day I was driven in sober sunshine, along the main highway and then off and down a rutted, straggly turning, into a clump of orange trees. There was a dog and a cat and a farmhouse, and a stooped, clear-skinned old man in a trilby, and I was led inside to a parlour and played records on what he called a graphophone.

Mr Schiller's forefathers had come out to the Barossa with the earliest settlers, and when he wished he could still speak in a quaint and stilted German, but still a German I could understand.

I sat on the hard-backed sofa in his Victorian parlour, listening to his graphophone and the ticking of the clock. And to him, talking. He told me about going all the way to Gawler, fifteen miles, in spring buggies, and then on by train to Adelaide for the Great Exhibition in 1910. He told me about the German nursery rhymes his mother used to sing him, and about going tin-kettling the night before a wedding — making a great din on saucepans and bowls and kettles, and singing outside the bride's house till she and the other womenfolk came out with beer and cakes.

'We made a noise,' he cackled. 'And we used to sing at 'em. "How dry we are, how dry we are, God only knows how dry we are . . ."' He had a paper-thin voice. 'Like me to sing to you?'

'Yes, please, Mr Schiller.'

'All right, wait a minute then.'

Where had he hobbled? To some cool, distant, clean part of the perfect farmhouse, with its glass cabinets full of dainty Victorian ornaments, and its hand-embroidered chairbacks and its clocks and its graphophone and its cat on the doorstep: a plump, white-bibbed tortoise-shell that had gone up and kissed the black dog on the nose.

Through the window I could see the boughs of the orange trees bending in the wind. The sunlight was beginning to weaken, dim and flicker. Soon this would be like every other wet and gusty day.

'Here we are!' Back again, mine host bowed beneath his cumbersome apparatus. In the centre of his neat, lacquer and needlework parlour, he was strapping himself into a public address system. Professionally, he blew down his mouth-organ. Then he tapped his foot. 'You brought a tape-recorder?'

'No, I'm sorry, all I've got is this notebook.'

'You could've made a *recording* of me. People come and make 'em, I do this a lot for them radio fellers.' Wrestling with the boa-constrictor public address, he produced and handed me a carefully printed card. 'Now that there's the list of titles. You just tell me what you want to hear.'

So I picked out *Tannenbaum* and *Stille Nacht* from amidst the phonetic spellings, and sometimes he sang, and sometimes he played a twinkling tune, with lots of spit. And the public address system broadcast his performance, and outside the window the cat and the dog joined in, and I applauded when he took a rest. He didn't take a rest often, and when he did it was to chant the children's hymns his mother had required with prayers before sleep.

Ich bin nur ein kleines Kinderlein
Und mein Kraft ist schwach.

Ich mochte gerne selig sein
Und weiss nicht wie ich es machen soll,
Und weiss nicht wie ich es machen soll.

There he stood, intent and concentrated, tapping with one foot, wrapped in the coils of the twentieth century and singing in a language that had come to the Barossa one hundred and forty years before.

When someone drove up to collect me, I shook Mr Schiller's parchment hand and touched his pink face, and thought of the enormous journey it had been for him, to go all the way to Adelaide when he was twelve years old. I would be back with Jill within hours. I could be back in London in a shorter time than it had taken him to travel from his home to the Great Exhibition. On an impulse, I kissed him: an old exhibitionist.

'What was it like? Did you enjoy it?' Jill and her family in a hub-bub, round the vast packing case of bottles.

'Yes, very much,' I said. 'But it rained a lot and I kept getting soaked and I feel a bit funny.'

'I don't like —' snapped the doctor.

'Yes, I know. My scar tissue.'

'Do you have lemons in England?' Andy craned round the door-frame to ask me.

'Yes,' I croaked feebly. 'Do you have tonsils in Australia?'

'Course.' He wriggled, nonplussed.

'Bet they aren't as big as mine.'

CHAPTER TWENTY-TWO

Not that I had them any more. And as I drowsily looked back on it, losing the rotten, swollen things had seemed such a very good idea.

Quite apart from clearing an airway so I could breathe and swallow some food, there'd been the week in a hospital bed. A rest from work, a rest from the flat (which was full to the brim with gas fitters, and pest control officials wondering whether plaster-beetles were pests), and a break from *everything* before I flew away. It really had seemed sensible. Like marriage or suicide or murder, it had seemed sensible at the time.

I had finished a manuscript at three a.m. on the day I was to be admitted, and presented myself with a small holdall in a sunny, deserted ward. All the removable patients had gone to their families for Easter, and wouldn't be back till that night. So I sat in bed, freshly bathed and examined, writing letters and reading novels, and then had a wonderful sleep. And the following day I enjoyed the pre-med (but then I invariably do) and was trundled, horizontal, through corridors and into lifts and out again and through swing-doors, and finally into an ante-room where sanitised fingers plucked at the name-tape on my wrist.

A voice in my euphoria said 'What about her adenoids?' and my brain cleared as though someone had sprayed it with Mr Sheen.

People will tell you that pre-meds make you sleepy. I am here to tell you that, threatened with extensive surgery, I can wake up from the brink of death. I sat bolt upright on the stretcher and screamed 'You're not touching my adenoids!'

'All right, all right,' soothed several white-masked figures. And I was shushed and told 'Tonsils, tonsils' and made to lie back down. I lay there, wide-awake and rigid, totally defying a backside-ful of dope. A terrible thought came to me, and being me I voiced it. I had seen *Hospital* and *M.A.S.H.* too many times.

'You're not going to rip anything else out! You're to leave my womb alone!'

'Womb?' squeaked a white mask. 'We'd have a job. This isn't the Channel Tunnel, this is Ear, Nose and Throat.'

'I know you lot.' I snuffled on my stretcher. 'Power-mad. A surgeon's knife in your ice-pack. Today, Ear, Nose and Throat — ' I waved my name-tape. 'Tomorrow, the world!'

One of the nurses began to giggle. One of the doctors began to giggle. An orderly choked on his mask. I was giggling so much the ceiling was going up and down. Somebody started laughing. Very, very loudly. It may have been me. I think I'd goosed the anaesthetist. Anyway, all of a sudden the little room was full of green-gowned people who'd come through from the theatre showing their eyebrows above their masks, and the young ones in white went quiet and docile, and somebody stuck a pin in my hand and that's when the ceiling fell down.

I won't dwell on what I felt like six hours later, when I woke up.

I won't dwell on the fact that the new post-operative theory isn't ice-cream, it's toast and cornflakes; and I wanted to get well so quickly to get off down to Australia that I forced down toast and cornflakes from the very first post-operative day. With nothing between the food and red-hot broken glass but a couple of Disprin every four hours. This for someone who takes Pentathol for a headache.

I will not dwell on crawling from my bed at four a.m. and begging a steely probationer for something for the pain, and being told to control myself. I controlled myself: I didn't kill her.

I will not dwell on the night when a young girl who'd had a serious ear operation started vomiting all over her bed just as I had a torrential nose-bleed and another patient began screaming for a bed-pan.

I will not dwell on the staff-nurse who looked down my throat and said 'They won't let you out of here.'

I will not dwell on the dressing-gowned man making milk drinks in our mixed ward, who turned down an orgy because he hadn't got the strength.

I will not dwell on these events, but I'll mention them, so you'll know what I've been through.

In Adelaide I dwelt on them, to a considerable extent. I dwelt on them, on paper, when I was sitting up in Jill's guest-room bed, catching up on my letters. I dwelt on them to Jill and her husband and her mother and Ben and Andy, when I was well enough to totter about in search of lemon trees.

I dwelt on them to Hester, who had heard me on a 'phone-in and eventually tracked me down.

And when my voice was better I dwelt on them to Audrey, whom I rang in Sydney (having reversed the charge). I shouldn't have travelled so soon after having my throat cut. There'd been far too much talking, and too much exposure to wogs. And now I was supposed to do more promotion in New Zealand; the publishers had bought a ticket, so I could call in there on my way home.

'Audrey,' I croaked. 'I can't do it, Audrey. No.'

'ALL RIGHT, DARLING. DON'T YOU WORRY ABOUT A THING. WE HAVEN'T GOT THE BOOKS ANYWAY, DARLING. WE'LL HAVE TO GET MORE NEXT TIME.'

'Audrey, you don't mean I did all that promotion for nothing?'

'NO, DARLING, OF COURSE NOT. THEY'LL

ALWAYS REMEMBER THE PUBLISHER'S NAME.'

'Oh, my *God* —'

'DARLING, YOU'RE UPSETTING YOURSELF. I CAN HEAR – ISN'T THAT YOU CRYING? IT'S NOT GOOD FOR YOU IN YOUR CONDITION. MY CHIROPRACTOR TOLD ME STRESS IS ABSOLUTELY THE WORST THING.

'Audrey, all I want to know is can I miss out New Zealand?'

'JUST STOP OFF FOR A HOLIDAY, DARLING. IT'S AS QUIET AS THE GRAVE.'

'I don't want to be buried, Audrey!'

'DARLING, IT'S THE *LIVING* DEAD.'

The pilot on the Quantas flight seemed to be in agreement. Over the Tannoy he said 'For s'vral hours now w've been over the ocean and, well, there hasn't been much to see. But, well, w'll soon be approaching Auckland, and y'can see even less.'

CHAPTER TWENTY-THREE

Auckland turned out to be a pleasant place in which to have a breakdown. Not, you must understand, that New Zealand was responsible. Melbourne was responsible: I'd found out I'd have to go back.

Again.

For the second time.

Through a conspiracy of calendars and airline schedules, it had proved essential to depart for New Zealand from Melbourne, a city that had all the attraction of Dachau for me. *And* I'd have to stay overnight, in order to make my connection.

Gritting my teeth on my scar tissue, I'd flown in with a low profile, booked myself into an hotel room and put a pillow over the 'phone. If the Australian Tourist Commission rang, they might be smothered by osmosis.

But they didn't ring, I'd kept my whereabouts successfully secret, and the following morning I presented myself at Melbourne Airport, frail but prompt. To be faced with one of those ticket clerks whom Woody Allen has spoiled for life. Short. Bespectacled. Optimistic – with no reason.

'Alida?' it said brightly. 'That's an unusual name.'

'Really,' I said, unsmiling. I could afford to be unsmiling. I wasn't promoting any more.

He leaned across his ticket desk. He must have been standing on something. 'My name's unusual too.'

'Is it really.'

'Yes.' He smirked. 'It's Paul.' A shy shrug. 'It's the way

I tell 'em.'

I looked at him. Obviously he was standing on his ego.

'Like to guess my middle name?'

'No.'

'My middle name's unusual.'

'No.'

'Guess and I'll give you a window seat.'

Impasse.

'Non-smoking section?'

I gave up. 'What's your middle name?'

'I thought you'd never ask me.'

'You were almost right.'

He leaned even farther over his counter. His glasses were pressed close against my eyelashes. 'My middle name's Vincente.' He waited. 'You know, like Vincente Minnelli?'

'Now can I have my boarding card, please?'

'It's unusual if you're Jewish.'

Grabbing my boarding card, I stalked off to find a coffee and found a friend, searching, instead. The very same journalist who'd ferried me out from town when I was in a dire condition. I'd written him a thank-you letter when I was recovering from the Barossa, and spent several paragraphs grumbling that I'd have to fly on through Melbourne. But I hadn't expected –

'I just think airports are bloody places if there's no one to see you off.' And there he was, with a grin and a moustache at this fearful hour of the morning, to keep me company and feed me coffee till the clipped loud-speakers announced my flight. When I entered the airless tubes of the Melbourne departure lounges, his was the last friendly face that went with me in the crowded memories of Australia. Typical of all the people who had held wide the country's doors for me. Typically kind, typically caring, typically generous with his time. Jill and her family. Audrey and Alex and their 'family'. John Wayne and his family of mountains. Lisa and Peta-Marie feeding lorikeets at the Gold Coast.

I arrived tired, sore-throated but buoyant in Auckland. It had been the experience of a lifetime, and now I was on my way home. Soon, soon, I could tell everyone all about it; Home Fires and my Mother first, of course, and specially. I'd written constant letters, but letters weren't enough. And the 'phone calls and the proposals had reached an average of three times daily, but nothing, and certainly not DIY, was really a substitute. Thank God, at least, to be away from Melbourne. Four hours on the 'plane – that was four hours towards my way back. The sun was blinding, the air was crystal, the weather was much better – *warm* – in New Zealand. Mind you, that wasn't hard. My friend the Melbourne journalist had stared out at the freezing drizzle and said 'It's so bloody cold here you can't even stand up in the bath.' Well, that was a world away now. I was going to like it in Auckland.

And then Ian Crysell, the publisher's local bloke who met me, suggested we confirm my onward ticket.

And I discovered that the flight to Singapore was routed via *Melbourne.*

Four hours' flying, back to that glacier.

Then a wait for a connection, and a seven-hour flight to Singapore.

This 'call in on your way home' lark was a geographic taradiddle, propounded because no one from England knew where New Zealand *was.* They all thought it was just up from Australia a bit. I could have flown direct to Singapore from Melbourne, been there two days earlier and saved myself a whole eight hours of air-conditioning throat.

In addition to calling a doctor, the local bloke had me watched by reception, in case I wandered away from the hotel and was never seen again. I went completely potty, and when I wasn't ranting and pacing I sat on my bed, quivering. In between the brandy I was taking four kinds of medicine, as well as the sleeping tablets which I sat and coughed up all night.

Amazingly, none of this could blind me to the beauty of New Zealand. I was taken out and shown it, as a form of therapy. Rather than fly back to Melbourne, I considered settling down. Beyond the sprawling straddle of Auckland, you looked across blue water to bluer, gently rising islands. The broken effect that the river had caused in Brisbane was here caused by the Pacific, and the Tasman Sea. Around the Hauraki Gulf and the Firth of Thames, deeper, the land formed a chipped and broken lobster claw. Though the land's brokenness was healed over by lush vegetation, and the rippling concrete sea that was the city of Auckland itself. From any vantage point it stretched, never-ending, undulating, its buildings touched and stripped by the all-seeing, ever-seeking light.

That night the local bloke rounded up some friends of his, either as moral support or potential ward orderlies, and we all went out to dinner and talked about my life. They asked me about my marriage and when I answered they thought I was joking, and when they found out that I wasn't they asked me soulfully if I'd really *tried.* Then they tucked me in my hotel room and went off to a Sauna, presumably intending to cement their marriages.

Next day it took two of the well-built ones to get me on to the aeroplane, and those who were still weak from the Sauna crouched and chipped my heels out of the tarmac.

Thank God, I told myself, stiff-necked all the way back to Melbourne, at last this was Singapore Airlines and all the drink I so needed was free. Stewards and stewardesses brought round steaming or cologne-soaked face cloths, and I wrung these offerings grimly, hoping to melt the rictus on my face. A meal, and the ocean beneath me — it could have been very enjoyable, if we hadn't had to come down.

Tensely, in the transit lounge, I studied the board listing departures. There was a British Airways flight leaving shortly for London, and I was seized with a desperate longing to switch to that homeward-bound 'plane. It would mean being back home tomorrow.

Home. The chaos of Heathrow. Not this, the one airport I had grown to loathe most in all the world. With outside permanent 'flu weather. With inside a modern concert hall. With life, after passport-control vinyl corridors, totally enclosed but broken by little pockets, where you sat, shifting, sticking to the clammy plastic seating, waiting for a flight that local trouble had inevitably delayed.

I unstuck myself to go and get a coffee, and found that the vending machines were all vending a low-calorie substance for the same price as a stiff champagne cocktail.

I would do it, I would: I'd change my ticket. No matter that the Proposer had been planning our reunion since before I left: had booked a suite into which to whisk me straight off the tarmac and was zeroing in on a date still a week ahead.

Nothing mattered. I couldn't stand this wretched, stuffy place one more minute. I would change flights and take extra sleeping pills and wake up in London. I would . . . As I skittered past it, the departures board flickered giddily. And an emotionless voice came over the Tannoy. British Airways regretted to announce a flight delay of twelve hours.

I trudged back to the group in the transit lounge pocket, and soon we were in transit for far Singapore.

The 'plane was crowded, and it wasn't long before the lady beside me was dozing. Unless I lay flat, or had a shoulder handy, I couldn't doze. Hour upon hour stretched ahead and I had to have something to do with myself. Something public and fairly socially acceptable.

Reckless with brandy, I decided to look up the front.

I asked a steward, he asked the captain and came back to fetch me. I could perch in the flight deck, an airborne treasure-room from the Arabian Nights. Sloping banks of emerald, instrument-jewelled panels, and ahead of us, as viewed through a visor, the flat darkness broken by the bright scatter of Alice Springs. The captain explained

ADJUST HERE.....
AND HERE

some of the instruments to me. He told me about the international distress-call frequency, and the weird, untraceable messages he had picked up. His crew were quiet, courteous, polite and very busy. When they got too busy I returned to my seat.

And was accosted by a gallant, white-haired gentleman. He'd chatted while we scuffled our shoes in Melbourne: a striped-trousered Australian engineer. If I wanted to stretch out and sleep, here were three seats beside him. They were empty and he wouldn't use them — he'd sit up and work. Yet another case of Antipodean true generosity. Gratefully, with a lump in my throat, I lay down. Gratefully I snuggled beneath the blanket brought by the steward. As we droned smoothly North-East I fell into a light, thankful sleep.

What — I woke from a dream that rats were crawling all over me, and gnawing lumps out of several of my choicest parts. It wasn't a dream! The gallant engineer was busying himself with work he'd never get paid for. From the information his nimble fingers had collated, he could have designed me a bra and a chain-link, extra-snug-fit cat-suit.

Leaping out of the seats, I swore and went to spend the rest of the flight upright, squeezing in beside the lady who was snoring. I could occupy myself by sorting and getting ready the various papers I should have to hand.

Weeks now since I'd needed half this documentation. Let's see . . . Tickets, yes. Passport, yes. Oh, Christ.

I sat there with a finger in my passport. My innoculation papers, where were they? Cholera and smallpox — surely I couldn't have lost them.

Oh, Christ. I froze and remembered. They were packed.

Right in amongst the books and the letters and notepads, tucked in sometime during my Australian safari. Not needed until now. They were in my cases. And my cases (I hoped to God) were in the hold.

'What happens,' I asked a steward, 'if you land without

innoculation papers?'

"Perfectly all right, Madam. It can be done for you on the spot, at the airport.'

I asked for another brandy and swallowed it, perspiring. My scar tissue was helping by trying to choke me to death. One way they wouldn't suspect a suicide.

When my own, homely G.P. had jabbed me for cholera I'd fainted. Not in his surgery: when I'd got back to the Wendy House. Where I'd promptly gone down with what felt like Asian 'flu. For twenty-four hours only, but it had been ugly. I'd been luckier with the smallpox: just an arm there I couldn't lift. If I lined up in the airport, the twenty-six thousandth victim for the same blunted needle, I'd probably wind up in bed, if not on a slab. I didn't want to die anywhere they'd bury me quickly. I'd been too influenced, too early, by Edgar Allan Poe.

I landed in a cold sweat, which gave way to a hot one. Outside in the night air it was eighty-one degrees.

Passport control was no problem. But health documents were, predictably.

'My certificates are in my luggage, and my luggage —'

'Tha'll be dounstess. You can go, unpack them and blin them back up here.'

I scampered down and waited, and then I collected my cases. And began a very, very humiliating process.

When I'd started out on my trek, nearly two months previously, layers of tissue had separated the layers of clothes. One case had contained dresses and blouses for a hot climate, the other the jumpers and trousers for wintry cold. Shoes had been in bags, oddments ranged round the sides or in the corners, books and papers pressed carefully at the bottom, crushable things laid lovingly on the top.

Now, two months later, the first thing to come out of one case was a pair of socks wrapped round a fossil rock.

After the baggage hall had been turned into a lingerie department, I finally found my health papers, rammed everything into the bags again, sat on the cases to shut them and hurtled upstairs.

Yes, that was right, they were all in order. Yes, I could go out into Singapore.

But everyone else who had been on my flight had left now, or been met, or joined some party, or disappeared. I had the name of the hotel into which I'd been booked, the address of the Tourist Board — I knew I should contact them, but in office hours. It was nearly midnight, all they'd known was I'd be arriving today, sometime. I couldn't expect another miracle like Sydney; Stephen arriving, a genie with a big car.

I trailed out to the taxi rank and a chubby driver heaved my cases, watched me into the cab, slammed the doors and drove off.

It was raining. At first that's all it was doing. Just raining. A relief in the heat — except that it didn't get cool. I smiled at the driver in his rear-view mirror. He had a little electric fan fixed to the dashboard and it spun and whirred and created a warm, sticky draught. He began pointing out things, and if I could have understood what he was saying it would have been quite informative, I'm sure. He could understand me, though. He had understood the name of my hotel: 'Aw, yeh, Olchald Load.' And he understood when I pantomimed fanning myself and said 'Hot!' Hot and damp. Very. But surely I couldn't be sweating *this* much? Dampness running over my scalp and down my neck? My God, I could feel it trickling from my elbows! Sweat? This much sweat?

This wasn't sweat, it was rain.

The driver and I were being soaked through as we sat there. With every single one of the windows wound up. His roof didn't leak, but nothing could have withstood the force of the torrent: there was a fullblown monsoon pouring down on us. We might as well have been driving underwater, and streams gouted through the sills of the tightly-shut windows.

We drew up outside my hotel, giving off a bow-wave,

and I fished in my swimming bag for the minuscule fare.

It was lonely, arriving in that magnificent hotel. The foyer could have comfortably accommodated the Albert Hall. Marble and lights, the smell of heavy French perfumes mixed with hair-spray and good leather. Porters; bell-boys everywhere in bright red jackets; a wide-awake, pretty receptionist, one of a line behind an immensely wide desk, who checked me in and handed me an enormous room-key. I followed the boy with the trolley, feeling bedraggled and shabby. Women in long, subtle dresses; sleek men in black. The lift hissed shut and open, and I followed the luggage down a dense and soundless corridor, past doors with their numbers in light above their porches, melting patterns of ochre and black in the walls and carpets. A door was opened for me and I walked into a beautiful room.

A cool, panelled room with soft, concealed lights and many mirrors. The panels were brushed aside to reveal walls of wardrobes, television sets, desks, cupboards and drawers. Doors led to bathrooms, lighted mirrors led to dressing-rooms. Draperies were parted to show me night-lit Singapore.

The boy bowed and vanished. And my telephone rang.

'Hey,' said the engineer. 'Y'said y'd be stayin' here. 'Fraid I lost y'at the airport. Like to come down f'radrink?'

I used an olde Englishe expression and hung up. And the 'phone immediately trilled again.

'Now, look!' I bellowed, and a strange voice said incredulously 'Miss Baxter?'

I hesitated. To *whom* had I given my name?

'Miss Baxter? I'm with the Singapore Tourist Board. My name's Simon — didn't you know I'd be coming out to meet you? I waited at the airport, I held up a card.'

'A card?

'I held up a card — we don't want people arriving to feel alone. Never mind, you got here all right? No trouble?'

'No, no. Of course not. My goodness — '

'May I just come up and leave you your itinerary? You can look through it and come along to the Office tomorrow. Sleep as late as you like. You must be very tired after that flight.'

'Yes, yes I am. Thank you.'

Five minutes later the doorbell rang in my quiet suite, and there was a young Chinese as drenched as I was. I'd wrapped a towel round my hair. 'It was raining,' I said feebly.

'Yes, it's the season. Here, you look through this and come along to the Office when you're rested. You got the address? Somebody'll take you out to lunch, take you wherever you want to go in the afternoon. You want anything, you just let us know. If there's anything missing from the itinerary, or if the itinerary's too much for you, just say. We want you to enjoy it here. Relax. Singapore's the place for a holiday.'

'Singapore's the place for a holiday.' I took the folder of papers and wiped them — they were dripping.

With a grin and a 'Good night, sleep well' the wet young courier went.

Beyond the windows the lights were mistily lovely in the downpour. A city. But not a scrubbed Western city. I was going to have a holiday.

CHAPTER TWENTY-FOUR

'You li' it?' asked Madeleine.

'Yes,' I said. 'What is it?'

She looked thoughtful. 'Iss a sor' of dumpling.'

'Yes,' I said. 'I can see that.'

The beauteous Madeleine had taken me out for a Tam-Sin lunch. Tam-Sin appeared to mean you could eat till you couldn't walk. At the circular tables around us extended families were seated, bent low over their chopsticks and putting away food by the ton.

I peered at Madeleine over my dumplings. With any justice, she'd be fat. But there wasn't an inch of surplus flesh on her supple, slender body, she had the sort of complexion that would make magnolias pout, and any time she walked through a paddy the rice would have steamed itself.

Madeleine on her own would have been sufficient reason for any man liking the Orient, but Singapore was full of her. Everywhere I looked there were shimmer-haired, wand-like young women with pretty legs and tiny feet and perfectly-manicured hands. They giggled continuously and necked with young men round transistors, and whenever their smiling lips parted they showed mouthfuls of white, even teeth.

I was dispirited, having got out of a taxi and fallen apart.

It's hard to accept, but there are some girls who are naturally beautiful. They do not need moisturiser or heated rollers or Vitamin E. They go to bed at night and wake up lovely in the morning, they eat like dainty hogs and yet they never put on an ounce, and no matter what they do they will always be beautiful.

And then there's the other kind: me.

Apart from my weight and the worry lines and the bags under my eyes there's the hair problem. My hair is very *English* hair — the sort that needs famine relief. I go into hairdressers and they rush about, moaning, with hot towels and conditioners and ask if they can cut it all off. Mine is not the sort of hair that looks best in humidity. I had taken it out of hairpins, combed it, got into a taxi, got out at the Singapore Tourist Board and found split ends dangling down round my ears. Two hours later a quick glance in the mirror told me that I seemed to be growing moss.

'Swee's,' said Madeleine briskly. 'I thin' you should try tha' dessert.'

'No, you can't mean it. I'm absolutely—'

'Bu' iss only coconut milk. They make it into a sor' of custard. Tastes li' vanilla ice-cream.'

'Oh, well—'

'An' what would you li' to do thiss afternoon?'

I pulled my waist together and opened my handbag. 'I've heard,' I said confidentially, 'that it's cheap to have jewellery set here.'

'Cheap? Iss very cheap. You wan' some jewellery?'

'No, but I've got this opal. It cost me practically nothing and it would be stupid to have it set in London because they'd charge me more than the stone was worth. I was wondering whether there'd be time to have it done here.'

'We'll as' — I'll take you to the People's Palace.'

Madeleine sprang up: one graceful, fluid movement. I hauled my bloated body to my boat-like feet.

The plump, bland ladies who had wheeled huge trolleys of selections between the tables went on trolleying and wheeling, and the extended families went on eating ceaselessly. Madeleine collected what we'd left in a big

DOGGY BAG
DRAGON BAG

doggy-bag.

Outside, my throat relaxed in the humidity – which was doing a whole lot of no good to my hair. There comes a time when you give up altogether. I wrapped a scarf round my head and stumped after my leader, who was swaying over monsoon drains in strappy sandals with spike heels. She leapt into the mini-van provided by her office, and I climbed up beside her and watched Singapore jolt past.

The city must have been the place that inspired Jack and the Beanstalk. It had orchids like acne and traffic-islands had sunk under pineapples. Pedestrians fought back the foliage to get on their buses, and if you didn't hurry the frangipani sneaked over the pavement, wound its flowers round your ankle and rooted you there, to the spot.

The previous night's heavy rain had left no trace behind it, for the heat had evaporated every sign of water from the ground, but the air was still moist, always moist, faintly sticky. To someone whose throat had dried up it was convalescing in Heaven. I belched discreetly. I really had eaten far too much at that unending Tam-Sin lunch.

The van rattled along through the heavy, tinny traffic, pulling up at the lights for the crossings that spanned the wide roads. Clusters of little girls in white blouses and pleated school uniforms hung about on one white-stockinged foot, giggling, swinging briefcases and then trotting briskly across. We drove past playing fields and the bright sports grounds of colleges, where boys threw themselves around beneath the hanging, spinach-green trees. Bushes and blossoming branches shaped every turning, erupting between high-rises and billowing from the concrete.

I didn't think I'd ever be able to find my way anywhere – Singapore was too full of different kinds of town – but then I wouldn't need to. I'd never seen so many taxis. And trishaws and rickshaws, wobbling with lovers and tourists; the bicycle men were sinewy, with short-sleeved shirts and bulging, hard calves.

Madeleine touched the simple gold chain at her throat – a decoration that in London would have cost several hundred guineas – and called to the driver that we were there. The People's Palace was a crammed and jostling shopping-centre: strings of jewellers' shops, every kind of store that you could wish for, and Madeleine suggested we should wander in and out of a few to compare prices. She herself had decided to look for a bracelet – 'Somethin' inexpensive, to massh this chain.'

In the third shop she found it, a jointless slither of gold the price of a pound of coffee. Less decisive, I plucked at a tray of ring-settings and nervously extracted one. A hoop into which the oval opal slipped and nestled neatly. Madeleine approved: 'Thass the best one. So simple.' And a girl behind a counter tapped out figures on a calculator, and said yes they could do it easily and the setting would be twenty-four carat gold.

'When by?' I squeaked, so shaken by the low price that I forgot to bargain.

'You wan' pic' irrup on your way th'Ellpolt?' And if they used less gold it would cost less than the price quoted, and anyway that price depended on the exchange rate. Same price Singapore dollars could be five pounds or twenty-five tomorrow. I feverishly considered my currency. How about Australian dollars? Her fingers flew over the digits: more promising than sterling. And New Zealand? A silence of dread fell on the glass counters of the jewellers. The banks had stopped dealing in New Zealand dollars. 'Oh, my God,' I said, 'what happened? Did they find out I'd been there?'

We left behind my opal, for which I was given an indecipherable but honourable Singaporean receipt, and Madeleine helped me back in the van and asked me what else I wanted to do.

I would be home in a few days. Ever since I'd started out, I'd been terrified of being left with no money. Apart from the opal and liquid refreshment, up to now I hadn't bought anything. This was the time, if ever, and weren't there all of those stories . . . 'Madeleine,' I ventured, 'is it true, about having dresses made to measure here?'

She gaped. Even gaping she was lovely. 'All clo'es are made to measure here!'

'But I mean — can you have them run up overnight?'

Madeleine leaned forward and twittered at the driver. Whatever she said, her mouth made shapes like a moving flower. We settled back in the van and I studied her ruefully. What a sin, I thought, that the local girls' looks went unmatched by the local men. Simon was as tall as me and quite nice looking, but I could have blinded the other men I'd seen with one hip. Most of them were very short and some of them were ugly. The rest were very, very short and *very* ugly. And to my horror, with them, being a woman didn't work. This was possibly because, set down beside the plainest local blossom, I shrivelled up and disappeared.

I sighed. There was no point in sighing too much about it; I'd just have to wear flat heels and keep a scarf round my moss.

It was a pretty little tree-lined street, and we were stopping. Madeleine stepped down and leapt nimbly over a grave-sized drain.

In a mélange of private houses, white-painted and swarmed upon by purple climbing plants, a glass-fronted shop stood out, filled with racks of dresses. I lumbered inside behind Madeleine and was formally introduced. Dresses? Before I left Singapore? I was instantly wreathed in tape-measures and dress-makers stood on each other to take down my higher details. The gloriously dainty owner stepped forward and began to tug at silk pleating, swoops of gathered jersey and crisply frothing cotton. I must try on a few styles first to see what suited me best. So I was stripped and piloted into a changing-room for Singaporeans, which was about the size of a wash-bowl and didn't even cover *my* modesty.

A sensation of material cascaded over my head. And I

walked out into the shop again, feeling very different. The weight and folding of the garments altered me. I had never moved in such silk-lined, superbly-cut clothing, every stitch sewn by hand and every stitch invisible. For years, until her patience gave out, my Mother had made everything I'd worn and my clothes had been made beautifully — but creations for sultry evenings, that needed nothing beneath them . . . fabrics that might have been melted and then, liquid, poured upon you . . .

Rounded, pearly-nailed fingers pulled here and there, and pinned. Someone got on the floor and estimated how much longer, and whether this would look better in black, or that, over there, in coffee. The owner would deliver two of the loveliest designs to my hotel room, but didn't I like this blouse also? And what about the line of this skirt, here?

Their customer was faint with desire but she had to live back home in London, and a few Nos said now in Singapore could save a lot of Nos said later at the bank.

The van and Madeleine returned me, sighing, to my hotel lobby. Simon would be picking me up for dinner, and we arranged that the following morning I'd be taken round the harbour on a junk. If only the better weather would continue — the sunshine was bright, and had been all afternoon.

I went upstairs to change into a bikini, and ran about opening and shutting cupboards and doors like a child. In the silvery bathroom there were sachets of bubble, and packets of bath-hats, and soap-powder so I could wash out my lingerie. There was an extension to the telephone, in the shower, and in the hall a 'fridge was full of iced drinks. Outside the windows Singapore stretched, rich and sunny, in green waves and grey roadways towards the water of the harbour.

I put a wrap over my bikini and took the lift down to the swimming pool. Towels were brought to me, big enough for elephants or even small boys; lounging chairs were dragged up; refreshments brought by perfect girls with sly smiles; and round the pool lay heavy Occidentals, dozing-like hippopotami. I was chatted up, mildly, by a lounging auditor, and took myself upstairs when the sun went down.

This was when, showered, cosy and bath-powdered in a towelling sheet, drinking the tea I'd ordered, looking out as the lights flickered on, I wished for somebody.

Singapore was lovely. Lovelier than I could possibly ever have imagined, exactly my kind of mixture of spicy smells and activities for the insomniac. Exactly the combination of crumbling antiquity, modern compromise and tat to make someone like me, from Soho, feel most alive and at home. With the moisture in their air, my glands were going down for the first time in weeks. I was warm all the time, and the air-conditioning was neither too hot nor too cold, and it worked.

If I could have stayed there, if by some miracle I could have brought those I missed most out to me . . . I'd rung home, and I'd spoken to the Proposer, and when he had rung me the telephonist had exclaimed 'Miss Basster? Hah, yess, all same soup?'

Tonight was one of those Eastern nights that don't stop at a promise. Given opportunity, and the slightest chance.

I knelt on a sofa and gazed, forehead pressed to a window. Why couldn't you ever have the right person in the right place at the right time? For so long I'd been travelling in such romantic places, but this was the worst – Singapore was rubbing aphrodisiac in the wound.

Oh, Hell. Half the time, minimum, I'd only wanted to be in London. All right, very soon I'd be there: wasn't that enough? The lights pulsated around the harbour. No, it bloody wasn't. And with my luck the minute I got back I'd start the curse. That had gone missing, vanquished in the onslaught of time-changes and antibiotics. The glass misted with my breath and I turned away.

They were running *Peyton Place* on the television. And *M.A.S.H*, two episodes, one straight after the other. I lay there thinking and let my tea get cold.

CHAPTER TWENTY-FIVE

Simon arrived with his sister to take me out to the car-park, and we stood in the lobby bowing and nodding and shaking hands. There were smiles all round and stifled fits of coughing: cautious of night-time mosquitos (once bitten, twice shy) I'd sprayed myself comprehensively with insect-repellent, and everyone in the lift had gone down with a little cough.

The Orchard Road car-park — Simon strode along, choking — was a famous place in Singapore. Packed with cars till six o'clock, when all vehicles were ordered away, and in came little carts, and tables and chairs and barrows, and suddenly the asphalt area was an open-air restaurant. Lights were strung, flaring, from the awnings of the food-stalls, reed-thin men flipped pancakes and stirred fish on greased hot-plates, women mangled sugar-cane and offered you tall glasses of frothing, misty green drink.

Every moment, at every barrow, you were embraced by chatter and a new smell: frying, prawns and lobster; steaming, vegetable- and meat-stuffed dumplings; fresh fruit, wedges of dripping pineapple, and oranges pressed and emptied for their juice.

Simon found us a table and hurried away to order — one dish from a barrow, two or three more from stall-holders and carts; a boy sent for long drinks and a child for tissue-wrapped sweets. All around us now, far fewer Europeans. Perhaps they had been scared off by the spluttering fat, the bursts of heat, the ramshackle mess of plastic-topped tables, the squawk of dialects, the damp, giggling faces . . . Perhaps it was much too far from their street-corner take-away.

I nibbled Saté from wooden skewers, dipping the ribbon squiggles of beef into peanut sauce and chilli. Simon smiled a lot and ate heaped noodles, pointing out the choice on the sizzling stalls in his American-accented perfect English. His sister was solemn-eyed, quiet and serious: a garbage-disposal unit in prim packaging. It took her, in *her* perfect English, an entire hour of eating to explain her computered job. I was swallowing Saté with a female Einstein.

Little boys came for the dishes and napkins and the brother and sister walked me back to my hotel. Full and idle, we stopped to browse in bright open shops: brooches in ivory, figurines in jade, orchids dipped in gold and captured for ever. An American woman behind me said 'D'you remember Sri Lanka, Mamie?'

I didn't want to go to bed yet, and wandered for hours in the warm night, but eventually I had to go — back to my hotel room, to midnight movies and sleeping tablets, to sleep and to waking to a bright, breezier day.

A car and Simon took me down to the harbour, where I jumped from a jetty to the wet planks of a junk. I'd pictured this as being a small craft, but it was as large as a pleasure-steamer, with rows of seating and a slit-skirted hostess who lisped a commentary over a mike from the bridge. Engines throbbed us away from the quayside, but out amongst the islands they would be cut out, the sails would be raised and the broad decks would quieten to the flap of canvas and the wooden hull's creak.

From the water, Singapore was an overpoweringly modern city. Tower blocks and grey masses of concrete, wharves and loading bays — the colour and fragmented alleys hidden by massive solids.

We chugged between the islands, spotting villas, and bathing beaches, and other craft — other junks. Two tiny

Chinese girls accepted sweets from strangers and the hostess told us over the microphone that 'the halbur iss at lease siss or seven phantoms deep.'

The engines stopped, and old men in sweat shirts, their tobacco-brown bare feet silent on the sodden decking, puffed at invisible dog-ends and cranked the sails up with a treadmilled winch.

The breeze riffled my moss-like hair, and hummed in my ears as I listened to Simon. He was telling me what each island was named. So many times he must have had to make this trip, take tourists about, show them round Singapore – always with the same politeness, and patience, and gentle humour.

'But doesn't it bore you? Surely, be honest!'

'No, it doesn't bore me. Just drives me crazy.' He sorted his papers and handed me a brochure. 'Sometimes – those French tourists –'

'Yes?'

'I don't know why they ever leave where they've come from. That's the only place they seem to like.'

He wouldn't elaborate then, nor later in the afternoon. Not till days had passed, and more excursions, and we were having dinner at Raffles. Maybe the evening and the floating music and the quiet, smooth service brought down his guard. Or maybe he knew my visit was over and I wouldn't be likely to snitch.

Raffles wasn't just an hotel, of course; it was an enchantment. A spell round what used to be the British style out East. Palm trees grew in a grassy, candle-lit garden, where you could dine and lift a wine glass to the stars, and musicians wheezed that inexpensive music Noël Coward was absolutely one hundred percent right about. Within the many-winged, Chinese-box-trick of a building, archways led to courtyards or swimming pools and marble corridors led to formal restaurants or bazaars or bars.

The manager had led us all over the place, opening the

doors of the Tiffin Room so that I could peep into its white ghostly interior, those peacock-backed chairs from a million 'thirties movies drifting slightly in the far shadows. Suites had been unlocked so that I could see the bamboo desks and settees, the double bedrooms, the dressing-rooms and bathrooms, the over-furnished old-fashioned comfort.

Polished wood panelling behind me . . . I sat beside Simon, spooning up my dessert. Wasn't there some myth that you ate less in the heat? I had eaten now in Chinese restaurants, Japanese restaurants, Malay restaurants, Indian restaurants — and was wondering whether the elegant dresses I'd bought would still fit. For a change, I'd had a traditional English meal.

'French tourists?' I prompted.

'OK.' Simon allowed himself to look mildly cross. 'You've seen what it's like here — they can't do enough for you at Raffles. Probably some of the best service in the world, the atmosphere's great —'

'Right,' I said, sniffing. I had been reduced to such 'Here's looking at you kid' handkerchief wringing that we'd had to leave the Palm Court for the music-less, straight-backed grill room.

'They said they didn't like it here — it was too British. I had a week with them, believe me. No murders — I don't know why not. They insulted everybody they met. Nothing was good enough for them, anywhere. Not as cool as France, not as warm as France, not as clean as France, everybody spoke English — Raffles? They *hated* it here.' He tapped at his cup. 'So . . . We were at a long table, twelve of them, all grumbling. And I said how sorry I was, that everywhere we'd eaten in Singapore they'd had to use chopsticks. I knew it must have been hard for them — and they went for me. And how. Didn't *I* think French people were *clever* enough to use chopsticks? Fine, I said. Nice to know you can manage. And I ordered them a T-Bone steak dinner. With potatoes and peas.' His spoon chinked on the saucer.

'Then they were all too proud to ask me for knives and forks.'

I sipped my coffee. 'More,' I breathed. There is nothing so congenial as a perfect person who turns out to have a breaking-point.

Simon was warming up now, he helped himself to more sugar. 'I took them on the junk cruise – you remember? Where we went the other day? And we stopped at one of the islands, but the island wasn't pretty enough. The beach wasn't big enough, the sand was yellow not *golden* – *on* and *on* and *on*. So I said, yes, but at least you can go nude bathing. And I ran into the sea with no clothes on. And they all did the same. Jesus Christ did they look ugly.

'I had my swimming trunks rolled up in my hand and I put them on when I was in the water. OK. There was a policeman – there's always a policeman – and he came running down to the water blowing his whistle and waving his arms and going crazy, and I walked out with my trunks on and there's these twelve French people huddled in there crying and screaming.' He tooled with his spoon. 'That was a week. It started badly. We gave them a party when they arrived, and one of our Tourist Board girls had to go up and pin flowers on everybody, and she pinned a flower on one of those French women's chests and her brassière started to hiss.'

That night, still in the long silk dress I'd put on to eat at Raffles, I was taken on a trishaw ride through the streets of Chinatown. Past the swarming temples, past the gossiping diners in the scented alleyways. Past the tables, and the pork and noodles, past the Indians stretched out on the pavements, fast asleep on their swept piece of ground. Past the running dogs and the small children with grease round their mouths. Past the stalls of tat and old records. Through the soy-scented night to the harbour, and the slight breeze from the sea, where the fabulous Merlion foamed water from its illuminated jaws.

Rattling across Singapore towards the airport the following evening, we passed the tourists and the Sate-vendors and stopped at the People's Palace so that I could dash into the jewellers and collect my ring.

'We din nee' so mush go' so iss only — '

And I had to swallow, not because of a sore throat this time but because I was leaving. I had never felt so torn in two. I was missing London dreadfully, aching with homesickness, wanting to get back and talk and tell everyone about what I'd seen, but Singapore was Soho with flowers and trees and a better climate . . .

The hot damp air breathed on my face as I walked across the tarmac. Simon had kept me company in the Silver Kris lounge till my flight was called, and now a pretty girl (of course, what else but pretty?) carried my packages into the bus that took us out to the 'plane. The buildings were indistinct beyond the bus windows: there was a mist. Would I leave in rain, as I'd arrived?

The Jumbo eased into the night, turning with dignity above the blurred shimmer of the harbour. A steward leant beside me, offering champagne and caviar.

And it was all too much, it had been too much for a lifetime. Too many friendly people, too much to do and too much to see. Too much sensation and too much emotion. Too far away – and thank God I was on my way home.

CHAPTER TWENTY-SIX

When was it exactly that I knew I'd really got there?

When I'd come down from my couch upstairs for my breakfast kedgeree, and a white-haired English gentleman turned to bellow 'The White Cliffs of Dover!' through a noseful of scrambled egg?

The chief steward brought us more champagne, into which I wept with gratitude – no, I still wasn't home yet. I was quite a way up in the air.

Was it when I stepped from the 'plane, lenses welling, and said 'England' to the Singapore Airlines chap who was carrying my hand-luggage? Shame he had to go back to his flight and leave me bearer-less in the Arrivals Lounge.

Could it have been when a porter ran his trolley over my instep and said 'If you doan bleedin' like it, bleedin'well go by train'?

Or was it when I hoisted a case, because no one else would do it, and my period started like the parting of the Red Sea?

Or when Home Fires and I missed each other in the chaos of the airport and I had to stand in a taxi queue in a state of panic and a tight white skirt?

No, surely it was later in the hotel, in the wrong room with the dirty cups and the full ashtrays, when the receptionist asked me who I thought I was.

'Don't you talk to me like that!' shrilled the receiver. Perhaps her bad temper was due to adenoids.

'But we've had this booking for over two months now,

and you've put me in this dirty room, and it's got *twin beds*—'

'Just because you want a double doesn't mean you'll get one!' And, once again: 'Anyway, who the Hell do you think you are?'

'Nobody.'

Not at home. But for two months I'd been made to feel rather special, and it was going to take me a while to get used to not being spoiled.

I sat on an unmade bed, chucking ticket stubs, envelopes and odd scraps of paper out of my handbag. A name caught my attention . . . Do you know, I never did ring that Queensland male prostitute.